Praise for Sandra Redding

"Sandra Redding has dedicated her adult life to writing and helping other writers along the path. She is a well-known, beloved teacher who has inspired and mentored many students over the years, including this one. Her writing is often humorous, always wise and filled with surprises. She has researched the story of Naomi Wise for many years, so I'm so pleased this project has come to fruition. Readers will enjoy this historical novel set in North Carolina."
Anne Clinard Barnhill
Author of At the Mercy of the Queen
St. Martin's Press

"Sandra Redding writes about ordinary people in an extraordinary way. With a narrative lilt reminiscent of Eudora Welty, she employs a delicate but sharp prose, and also like Welty, she shares with the reader the darkest sorrows and deepest desires of her characters, making us privy to their secrets. With a keen ear for dialogue and a meticulous eye for detail, Redding continues to paint our crazy Southern landscape with a fine brush."
Kathryn Etters Lovatt
2013 Prose Winner
Individual Artist Fellowship
SC Arts Commission

NAOMI WISE
A Cautionary Tale

Historical Novel

Also by Sandra Redding

Greensboro and Me: Dancing Through The Decades
A Memoir

Greensboro: Portrait of Progreee

Winston-Salem: Bright Star of the Future

*For Sharon
With gratitude —*

NAOMI WISE
A Cautionary Tale
Historical Novel

Sandra Redding

Sandra Redding

Alabaster Book Publishing
North Carolina

This novel is a work of fiction. Names, characters, and incidents are either the product of the author's imagination or are used fictitiously. Any resemblance to actual persons, or events, is coincidental.

Copyright 2013 by Sandra Redding

All rights reserved. Printed in the United States of America. No part of this book may be reproduced in any manner whatsoever without written permission except in the case of brief quotations embodied in critical articles and reviews.

Published by Alabaster Book Publishing
P.O. Box 401
Kernersville, North Carolina 27285
www.PublisherAlabaster.biz

Book and cover design by
David Shaffer

Cover photo by Joe Redding
Naomi Wise's tombstone remains in the cemetery at
Providence Friends Meeting,
Randolph County, North Carolina.

First Edition

ISBN 13: 978-0-9860300-3-1

Library of Congress Control Number
2013942437

Acknowledgements

To write this book required the help of many experts. Both Greensboro Public Library and the Randleman Library provided all books and materials requested and their savvy staffs answered endless questions.

The Friends Historical Collection housed in the Hege Library of Guilford College made me feel at home as they brought volume after volume of early Friends records which I eagerly perused, learning all I could about the early Quaker communities of Piedmont, North Carolina.

Thanks, especially to Louise Hudson, former Randleman Librarian and now Board Chair of the Randolph Historical Society Collection housed in St. Paul's Methodist Church in Randleman. Besides helping me locate archived materials relating to Naomi Wise, she shared many enlightening historical stories.

For continued encouragement during this and all writing projects, I offer gratitude to Kathryn Etters Lovatt and Ann Clinard Barnhill. The three of us have joyously shared writing struggles and successes for over three decades.

I also owe an appreciative shout out to my Critique Group, Seena Granowsky, Pat Jackson, Janet Shoffner, Elida Vinesett and Nancy White.

Last but certainly not least, heartfelt kudos to my husband Joe who willingly pitched in, making it possible for me to complete and publish the novel I always wanted to write.

Dedication

To my lifetime companion, husband Joe, and my two extraordinary sons, Joseph Benjamin Redding, Jr. and Michael Kent Redding. Thank you for tolerating my obsession with words. I love the three of you even more than I love writing.

One

Mary Ruth Eversole's Account of Naomi Wise
- begun June 1841 -

G athering up paper, India ink and the quill pen my eldest son Davey made from a turkey feather, I opened the door of my Randolph County farmhouse and hurried outside this morning.

Sunlight already drips through tree branches. The scent of lilacs stirs on a breeze. How easy it would be to lollygag, savoring the sights and sounds of early summer, but my heart binds me to a nobler task.

My plan, ambitious for certain, is to come here each morning, writing down the sad but true account of Naomi Wise, the orphan who nearly thirty years ago, a time when I was barely more than a child myself, came to our farm to help with cooking and housekeeping. While on this earth, she worked, as well, alongside my husband Garland Eversole, planting wheat, cotton, beans, corn, yams and squash. The poor child rarely complained, not even when tending messy chickens, but she did avoid the wild hogs roaming our land.

All who lived here in our small Society of Friends community knew of her. Most still recall the words describing her downfall—*Oh, Omi, who wasn't wise/ got took in by a mustached man/ spinning sticky lies/ down by the riverside.*

As I sit here, thankful for the blessed shade of the chestnut tree, the most valued tree on our property, I pray for God's help before I begin. Pausing to summon up the right words, I observe squirrels lured here by falling nuts. Deer, fox, even bear stalk the wooded areas, sometimes venturing onto our property. A few of the Friends in our society, those who arrived decades ago, claim that in the mid-1700s, a few buffalo still inhabited Randolph County. Thankfully, I was spared the fright of ever encountering those odd looking beasts.

Before my husband died, he shot many a creature nibbling in this spot. Yet, God forgive him, he sorely resented the attention I paid to this chestnut tree as well as to the colorful wild flowers growing so abundantly here. My propensity for beauty perplexed his Quaker heart.

Tis true, I veer a bit from our community's emphasis on plainness. Oh, I dress simply enough, always wearing a shift in a muted shade of brown over my corset, and, of course, a white apron as well as a white modesty piece around my neck to hide my chest. My small feet are shod with sturdy black leather shoes, and on my head, I keep a mob made of cotton to protect my hair while tending an open fire. Though this traditional clothing is sometimes uncomfortable, I am grateful for it. Especially my mob, for we women seldom wash our hair, particularly during the cold days of winter.

Despite my plain clothes, I'm still drawn to pretty things—a blue bird's nest filled with tiny eggs, a feather from a peacock, or the finely stitched quilt Naomi once made for me, the one formed of bold green, blue and purple patches now covering my bed, providing solace despite the chill of dark memories.

How I wish Naomi could have embraced plainness. It might have saved her, but when I behold the glorious redbud trees, now in full bloom, my heart, too, succumbs to all that's delicate and bright.

Indeed though few other women in the community ever praised her for it, Naomi's loveliness rivaled nature's splendor. Despite the grime beneath her fingernails and that head of tangled hair, I immediately spotted a beguiling sparkle in her dark eyes on the warm June day in 1800, the very first time I beheld her. She stood proud. No head hanging for that one, though she had doubtless witnessed more meanness than most children could endure. She wore a moth-eaten dress and the tops of her shoes, completely worn through, revealed crusty toes. Though she was barely twelve then, I fancied her avid stare attested to a keen awareness of the sights and sounds around her. Did I glimpse fear in her eyes? Sadly her brazen gaze almost convinced me none existed, but, as I learned later, particularly for survival's sake, Naomi's eyes as well as her bow-shaped lips lied.

I had stooped down that day to pluck daisies for myself and Nellie Haskins, the widow woman living next door. Nellie had been our neighbor since my husband and I traveled here from Pennsylvania in 1794. Newly wed, we trusted God and the red clay earth to provide all we might need. Those outside our faith considered our community peculiar, for unlike most North Carolinians, Friends opposed slavery and war. Peaceful folk, we usually stayed to ourselves relying on one another.

After hearing footsteps, I looked up into the pleading eyes of the unkempt urchin. When I handed her a daisy, the corners of her lips slowly responded, twisting upward. Nothing about her appeared familiar. No, her skin was definitely too dark to be one of us. Keyauwee Indians had once settled in the area. Perhaps their blood coursed through her veins, but, if so, not enough to make her full-blood. Could her parents be gypsies? Occasionally we heard rumors of tribes moving through North Carolina.

"M'am," she said. "Could you spare a crust of bread for a poor orphan child?"

Hearing the word orphan touched a cord. I had birthed two children, one born too early to survive; the other, a full-term girl who failed to take a single breath before leaving us. To keep tears at bay, I bit my lip so hard it hurt. I reached out, but stopped short of embracing her, for didn't I owe it to my husband to protect myself from diseases that might course through her thin body? At least her color was good, not pale and wormy. "What's your name?" I asked.

"I'm Naomi. Naomi Wise. I live over yonder, on the other side of Deep River. My maw lived up in Hyde County. After she took sick with a bad cough, they brung me here to live with my uncle."

"How old might you be, Naomi Wise?"

"Twelve."

Though obviously poor, there was about her a sense of entitlement. And with a bit of cleaning up and decent clothes, the child might actually be presentable.

"Where is your uncle now?"

She moved the toe of her shoe side to side before answering. "He gone hunting with kinfolk."

"What happened to your father?"

"Ain't never had one to speak of, M'am."

I closed my eyes to still my heart. "I'll see what I can find."

A few minutes later, I handed her a tin plate filled with warm field peas, alongside a triangle of cornpone. I pointed to a tree stump. "Eat there. I'll fetch water."

As I lowered a gourd dipper into the bucket, I wondered what the orphan's story might be. Since I knew nothing of her uncle, except that he wasn't one of us, a member of the Society of Friends who met once a month to meditate and wait for God to speak to our hearts, he most probably would be one of the men who came from the Eastern edge of North Carolina, those men with loud voices and booming guns, boisterously invading this peaceful Eden we called home.

By the time I returned, she'd already cleaned her plate. She didn't speak. Instead we eyed one another like two suspicious dogs, deciding if we'd come upon friend or foe.

"You have an interesting name. Have you heard the Bible story of Naomi? She was a virtuous woman, a woman much loved by her family."

"Maw said she liked the sound of it. That's why she gave it to me."

"So, you've never read the Book of Ruth?"

"No M'am. We had a Bible once, but Maw give it back to the traveling Preacher man."

"I'd be more than willing to share the story with you."

She toed the dirt with her foot again and wiped her runny nose on the sleeve of her shabby dress. "I ain't supposed to be here. If I'm not back before my uncle, he'll whoop me."

When I noticed the red marks covered her thin legs, I bit my lip and looked away. "I'd be happy to share the story anytime you want to drop by. Naomi and her daughter-in-law Ruth had a special relationship. They loved and trusted one another."

A butterfly landed on Queen Anne's lace growing nearby. Grinning, the child chased the fragile creature, squealing with delight until the insect turned, heading for her outstretched palm. I held my breath as it remained there for a few seconds, pumping exquisite wings of yellow elegantly edged in black. Naomi stood still as a post until the butterfly flew away once more. As if celebrating the moment, the orphan sang, "Lavender's blue, dilly dilly; Lavender's green, dilly, dilly..." in a high sweet voice. She continued to leap about, and then circled, turning around until collapsing on a bed of clover. Looking up, she giggled.

For that brief while, I completely forgot she was a poor orphan totally lacking prospects. With the butterfly clinging to her hand, she'd appeared utterly charming, poised, in charge.

Because Naomi did not ask my name, I did not reveal until later that I went by Mary Ruth. But that day, looking across my yard, where buttercups and sweet smelling honeysuckle grew in abundance and elm and birch trees were so tall they seemed to be touching heaven, I thought of the most quoted passage in the Biblical story, the reply that Ruth made to Naomi: "Whither thou goest, I will go; and whither thou lodgest, I will lodge...." I recalled making that vow to my husband Garland twice. First, when we married and again when we sojourned to this wilderness in a covered wagon, bringing our hoes and strong backs to tame the land.

Even before Naomi showed up that day, Garland had already gathered crops and milked our two cows before leaving to take a wagonload of corn to Dicks Grist Mill for grinding. By the time he returned, Naomi had left and I'd cooked greens in the black pot hanging over the fireplace. We'd have them with the leftover field peas and pone.

At mid-afternoon, as we enjoyed our last repast of the day, I spoke of the hungry orphan girl who'd come calling, attempting to share with Garland every detail. After I finished, he reached out, his large capable hand covering my fingers. "Don't do this, Mary Ruth."

Though handsome, with hair bright as the sun and eyes blue as cornflowers, Garland's expression changed. Frown lines made his face appear almost grotesque, as he warned, "Stay away from the child. She doesn't belong among us."

Tight lipped, I gathered our plates. After scraping them loudly, I dropped both into a pan of water. Garland came up behind me, wrapping his strong arms about my waist.

"Helping others," I asked, "Isn't that what we've been put on earth to do?"

Unusually silent and reflective, words often came hard for him, but finally they tumbled out. "Yes, we should most certainly aid others, but we also have a duty to protect ourselves. You do realize, don't you, that a girl from across the river can never be a daughter to you?"

How I resented his reading my heart. The stink of collard greens rose up, sickened me. Rushing outside, I threw up. As I retched, clutching my stomach, I spotted a young rabbit crouched, unmoving. Isn't that what I'd done for far too long, never moving, never causing a ruckus, simply remaining still to survive.

Needing to escape, I rushed heedlessly to the shore of Deep River, located less than two miles beyond our property. Gasping for breath, I settled on a large boulder near the water's edge. Usually, this was a comforting place, but due to recent rains, dark water tumbled around me. Shadows formed. I heard a low moan. Was it a woman? Perhaps some helpless child. Looking up, I watched the curved sickle of a new moon slice through the pitch black sky.

Shrieks and screams came from the woods. Perhaps only wind I wanted to believe, but soon my imagination transformed the noise into the sobs of children. Children without food. Children with worn-out shoes. The low moans of mothers searching for their lost ones joined in. As sounds reverberated in my head, I wrapped my arms around my knees, weeping for all of them as well as my own empty womb. That evening, witnessed by a thousand stars, I also wept for my husband, a good Quaker man, the person I loved most but rarely pleased.

Two

During the following week, I couldn't forget Naomi. One breezy afternoon, when I spotted a yellow butterfly on a bush, I recalled how wildly exuberant the child had been as she chased one around the yard. I remembered, too, her glee as she watched brown squirrels scampering on the limbs of the chestnut tree. One of them, as if in a trance, had stopped, curiously examining her.

How I ached to talk again to Garland about the child, but whenever I attempted a conversation, he headed outside to attend to one of his many chores. Particularly now that crops were coming in, his habit was to rise before daybreak. In addition to looking after our horse, two cows, as well as the pigs and chickens running wild on our land, he tended to the cotton, wheat, and corn as well as the food crops. I'd be a nuisance if I bothered him.

Deciding to seek an audience elsewhere, I took fresh churned buttermilk next door to Nellie, my ailing neighbor. Since she'd lost most of her teeth, she enjoyed softening her cornpone in it.

Nellie would be seventy-five her next birthday. Until two months ago, she'd been spirited and busy; now barely able to walk, she was down in her back. "Feeling poorly" is the way she characterized her illness, but during my last visit, I noticed serious changes: her color, almost yellow as a buttercup, concerned me. Her breathing was raspy, and speaking required great effort.

Nellie and her husband Jasper Lawson were the first to greet me and Garland when we arrived here, our covered wagon filled with feather beds, cooking utensils, water buckets and the tools we'd need to clear the land.

What an adventure it had seemed before we left Pennsylvania for this wilderness back in 1795 so we could join other Friends who had already migrated to this place where they might worship without being chastised. Only nineteen back then and perhaps a bit spoiled, I never envisioned how difficult cutting our way through wilderness or locating food and water could be. Though exhausted from the bumpy ride during the day, peaceful sleep never came at night. Howls of wild animals woke me. Terrifying dreams flashed through my mind. By the time we arrived, my hair was filthy and matted. Scratches from briers covered my face and arms.

As soon as Nellie introduced herself, I grabbed her around the neck and sobbed.

I surely wouldn't have survived without her. Before my first day in Randolph County, she soothed my addled brain with comforting words and my sore aching feet with lemon-scented liniment.

Most of the women in our community believed Nellie had been granted the gift of knowing. How could I doubt it? During our first year there, she and her husband advised where our home should be built to avoid flood waters and make use of the best light. Then they assembled with other Friends to help us build a log cabin with two large rooms separated by a chimney plus additional space up a short flight of stairs. During the second year, Nellie located water beneath the ground by holding out a forked tree limb she called a dowser. On the site where it vibrated, we found our well.

As I passed through the doorway of my friend's small tidy cabin, I called out. Nellie lifted her hand in greeting. Her hazel eyes, though tired, still radiated fortitude. As I settled myself in the straight back chair by her bed, I inhaled the soothing scents of lavender and thyme. Fragrant herbs always hung from the rafters of Nellie's place. I rested my fingers on her forehead. "You feel warm."

She brushed my hand away. "Don't be concerning yourself on my account."

I smiled, glad to see her feisty, but then, noticing that the yellow cast of her skin, I turned away.

"What have you come seeking?" she asked.

"Just to see how my dearest friend is weathering."

"Isn't there something else?"

Her question alarmed me, for I did have another motive. "Have you heard of a child named Naomi Wise?"

Perhaps, Nellie hadn't heard me, I decided, so I asked again, mentioning this time that Naomi lived on the other side of the river with an uncle.

She frowned. "Oh, well, she must be one of them from down East. From all I've heard those men spend most of the day shooting and drinking. Some say they abuse their womenfolk."

"Such rumors have made their way to my ears, Nellie, but how can we be certain? On this side of the river, we keep to ourselves, never visiting, never being visited."

"Oh, some of them used to come calling, all right. They

would've taken all the grain and cash Bonnie and Alan Mabry owned if Alan hadn't pulled a gun on them. A few nights later, one of his horses went missing."

Her response shocked me. How unlike her to be so uncharitable. "But Naomi's a child," I mentioned. "She surely deserves our help."

Nellie took my hand and stroked it with her gnarled fingers. "Don't fool yourself, Mary Ruth. Blood most often wins out. Although we say children are empty slates when they enter the world, her slate's already been wrote on. Probably several times and the words written ain't likely to be pretty."

"If what you say is true, it's even more important to find some way to help her."

"How does Garland feel about such thinking?"

I lowered my head. "I fear he thinks I'm searching for a substitute for the children I lost, but I'm not. How could anyone replace those innocent babes, yanked away and taking my heart with them? "It's just not fair."

She pulled her hand, puffed up with snaky blue veins, away from mine. "Dead babies are not new. Almost all the women in this place have lost at least one. Alison and Mabry Dixon lost ten, so don't let sorrow linger in your heart, Mary Ruth. Find a way to let it go."

I turned away, resolving not to cry. "I'd better get home. Garland shot two full-grown rabbits yesterday, so I'll be cooking us some stew. Hard as he's been working, he needs substantial food. Would you like me to bring you some?"

"No sane person would refuse your stew, my Dear." Her smile revealed toothless gums. "When will you be sharing your recipe with the rest of us?"

I took her question to be an accusation. She wasn't the only one who'd asked. Perhaps it was selfish of me, but something in my nature demanded that I hold back a few things from the other women. The stew recipe had been passed down from my German grandmother to my mother and then to me. If ever blessed with a daughter, the secret would be hers. Until then, I intended to keep the ingredients mum.

How Garland resented my need for privacy. I wondered if Nellie did as well.

"For my eighth birthday, my mother made me a corncob doll," I said to my friend, hoping that sharing the story would provide some insight. "It wasn't a pretty thing at all, but the doll—I named her Ivy—was mine, all mine. I couldn't bear sharing her with my sister, so I hid her in the barn."

Nellie, shaking her head, managed a smile.

"Over the next few weeks, rats must have gotten to my pretty doll and pulled out most of her hair. Still I loved her and vowed to keep her always."

"I suppose we all need something strictly our own, my Dear," she said. "But be careful. Unspoken words weigh down the heart."

I bent, kissing her forehead. There was about her a smell akin to moldy cheese. I didn't care for it. Against my lips, her skin felt clammy. "Sure you're all right?" I asked.

"Fine as a fiddle." She looked away then, out the window where dark clouds gathered. Again noticing the yellow cast of her skin, I felt certain my friend lied about her health. Still, didn't she own the right to her secrets just as I owned the right to mine? Smiling, I promised to come back later. "When I do, I'll bring sassafras tea as well as rabbit stew."

"Anything to warm my blood would be appreciated."

Busy the rest of the day, I washed dirty clothes in the river and spread them on large rocks to dry. Later I sprinkled feed across the meadow to attract the chickens. Garland stayed busy as well. When the sun finally set, I was so exhausted I pure forgot to check on Nellie.

In late afternoon, Garland and I, both bone tired, went up the stairs before the sun set. I expected him to fall asleep soon as his head touched the bed, but instead he pulled me to him, his strong arms holding me near. Then he tentatively caressed my breasts, making sure I was willing before entering me. How long it had been since we'd made love that way, sweetly and innocently, tinged with longing, yes, but also deep respect.

"I need you," Garland whispered in my ear.

"And I, you," I answered.

When he asked, "Do you really, Mary Ruth?" I was surprised, for I loved him with all my heart. Though we didn't always agree and though we didn't always share every thought, I couldn't imagine life without him.

The next morning, awakened by the cooing of pigeons, a deep contentment filled me. The closeness I'd experienced with Garland was much more than a mere physical bonding. I hummed an old song about a willow tree, one my mother had taught me, as I prepared my husband a hearty breakfast of salt pork and hoecakes cooked over an open fire.

As we ate, Garland was shy with me, and I with him. It occurred to me that we were acting more like newlyweds than a couple who'd lived together for five years. Before he walked outside, he named all the chores he hoped to accomplish. "And you, Mary Ruth, how will you spend your day?"

"I need to check on Nellie. I promised to bring her some of the stew I made last evening. Maybe it will perk her up."

After my husband left for the field, I rushed outside. A cardinal, red as holly berries, sat on a limb of the large chestnut tree. Closing my eyes, I made a wish. When I opened them, I waited impatiently for the bird to fly away. If he flew up, my wish would come true, according to the superstition my mother had passed on to me. Finally relinquishing the limb, the pretty feathered creature dipped briefly, but then soared up again.

Encouraged, my heart soared as well. Perhaps I'd spend my day doing what I wished to do instead of tending to usual chores. Hanging onto that thought, I quickly rearranged my plans. Taking a basket from the shelf, I filled it with a pottery crock of rabbit stew, and tied up at least two dozen shelled chestnuts as well as the leftover hoecakes in a napkin. I also added some of the sprigs of dried lavender and rosemary Nellie had given me and the corncob doll I'd held onto since childhood. The last item placed in the basket was my Mother's Bible, its black leather cover faded by time.

Three

Though fully understanding where my duty lay, I selfishly ignored responsibility. Instead of looking in on Nellie, I left my own house and my own people. Crossing the rough wooden bridge spanning the river, I callously sought what lay on the other side without once pondering my responsibilities to my husband or the Friends community.

I will not claim my walk through life has been a straight path. I have often veered too far right or left, briefly tramping through nature's wildness. But the day I sought out the orphan, I became bolder and, I suppose, more foolish than ever before. Still I refused to believe then and even refuse to believe today that wanting to see Naomi defied the tenets of my faith. Indeed, it was just the opposite, for the teachings of our Friends' founder, George Fox, instruct that we've each been given a great gift, a light inside that guides us, letting us know what's right. For two days the light within had pulled me toward the orphan. How could I keep ignoring it? To do so would be denying the light. Wouldn't denying the light be denying God?

My sojourn began as an act of faith dogged on by intuition. She will be there, my heart told me. Still, I'd expected to find her inside her uncle's cabin, wherever that might be, not outside squealing like a hungry pig as she pulled clumps of clay from a mud hole. Though I remembered her as a pretty girl, all evidence of my former opinion had disappeared beneath the streaks of mud covering her hair, face and clothes.

"Naomi, whatever are you doing?" I asked.

Without apologizing or explaining, she looked at me with those determined brown eyes. "Did you come to tell me the story of Naomi and Ruth?"

I laughed. "Certainly not. There'll be no story for a mischievous girl who plays in mud puddles."

My refusal obviously stunned her. "I'll be making something with the clay."

"Really? And what do you propose to make?"

After standing, she adopted a more respectful tone. "A pretty bowl or maybe a flowerpot."

"If you can find a way to clean yourself up, I'll let you have a look in my basket."

"There's the river."

"Take this," I said, picking up the large white cloth I'd used to cover items. "Once you get the dirt off, if that's possible, use the cloth to dry."

Dutifully, she walked away, finding a low path embellished on either side with soft ferns. Following along behind, I watched as she walked to the end of the path and continued toward the gurgling water.

Be careful I called as her filthy toes reached the water's edge. "There's a reason this place is called Deep River."

Though the day was warm, I shivered as I gazed out across

the treacherous water. I'd heard tales of people dying there, their bodies slashed open by the menacing rocks less than a few feet beneath the surface. Fearful for Naomi, I warned again, "Watch where you step."

"I'm not scared," she yelled back, boldly walking into the rushing water until her head disappeared.

I held my breath. But only a few moments later, she appeared again, splashing wildly. After playing in the water until the dirt dissolved, she used the cloth I'd handed her. By the time she walked from the river, she certainly looked cleaner, though by no means presentable, as she rushed, still soaking wet, to the large rock where I sat. I offered her a handful of chestnuts. She grabbed them and greedily ate every one.

"Now will you tell me bout Naomi?" she asked.

Taking my worn Bible from the basket, I turned to the book of Ruth. Was I being foolish? I wondered. Would she even comprehend the words? After I read several passages, I paused, glancing at her. Her eyes were intense, her small, well-formed hands folded in front of her stomach.

"First, I want you to know that Ruth is my second name; Mary is my first."

"So, is this story about you and me?" she asked.

"Not exactly, but it's a story about two women helping one another. Naomi was the older one; the younger, Ruth was her daughter-in-law. Naomi's husband died; later Ruth's husband died. Naomi planned to return to her own people. Since she and Ruth were from different tribes, she suggested that it would be wise for Ruth to stay with her own kind, but Ruth refused, saying "Whither thou goest, I will go; and whither thou lodgest, I will lodge: thy people shall be my people, and thy God my God."

"Was Ruth an orphan like me?"

"Oh, Naomi, I don't think so. Still the story demonstrates that two women from very different backgrounds can love and trust one another. Ruth considered it her duty to look after her mother-in-law."

When the sopping wet child stood up, I noticed mounds of breasts pushing against her wet dress. Almost a woman, yet she knew so little.

Sitting there, warmed by sun, we both relaxed. Taking in the beauty of the river, we watched fish jump up and small turtles, all in a row, line up on a log, making no movement except their heads going back in their shells whenever disturbed by the slightest noise. Finally Naomi's dress began to dry. Does your uncle ever take you fishing?" I asked.

"He shoots fish," she said matter-of-factly. "He says getting them on a hook takes too much time."

When I told her I'd brought rabbit stew for both of them, she turned from me. "Maybe we should take the things in my basket to your house," I suggested.

"I have no house." Her mouth turned down as if she'd bitten into something bitter. "It's uncle's house. If I had anywhere else to go, I wouldn't stay."

"Is he cruel to you?"

"I have to do whatever he says."

Her words troubled me, but as Nellie and Garland both pointed out, her people were not my people, so what could I do?

"Please, show me where you stay."

"All right. But Uncle's not home."

The exterior of the small two-room cabin was in sad shape. One corner of the roof had caved in. Quite different from

Naomi Wise A Cautionary Tale

the neat looked-after houses in the community where I lived.

Naomi reached out, taking my hand. Once inside, I was pleasantly surprised to see that despite the exterior shabbiness of the place, there were no spider webs draping from walls. Steam rose from a pot of beans hung over the fire, providing a comforting scent. I noticed a small rickety table held a crude clay pot. In it were a few droopy violets. "How pretty," I said to Naomi.

"I made it myself."

I touched her hair. "You're amazing," I told her, meaning it. "I really would like to speak to your Uncle. I want to tell him how proud he should be of you."

"He won't be home til late."

Though I hated to leave her, I knew I must. Garland had no idea where I'd gone, and I'd failed to check on Nellie. Though I'd hoped to see the uncle and thus gain a greater understanding of the child's situation, there was simply no way I could remain. Garland would be furious that I'd come at all.

Naomi insisted I have tea with her before leaving. As she poured it into a chipped cup, I walked to the doorway of the other room and glanced inside. Messy bedding covered a cot, the only other furniture a straight back chair and a dilapidated trunk. When I sniffed, I realized it smelled of whisky and rot. "Naomi, where do you sleep?"

When she answered, "On the floor, not far from the cooking pot," I was relieved.

Taking each item from the basket and placing them on the table, I waited until last to show her my Ivy doll.

"Ain't never had no doll before." she said.

After drinking the last of the bitter tea, I let her know I could stay not a minute longer.

When I bent to lift the basket from the floor, she wrapped

her arms around my waist, hugging me. "Now, you take care of yourself, Naomi Wise, and stay out of mud holes," I scolded.

She laughed, a raucous sound that I wouldn't soon forget. Then taking my hand, she said she'd walk me far as the bridge. When we came to the squeaky wooden boards dividing my people from her people, I walked slowly to the other side. A few minutes later, I heard sounds behind me. My heart pounded. Turning, I was relieved to see Naomi holding a droopy daisy in her hand.

As I hurried home, I decided to confront my husband, telling him something ugly and mean was happening to Naomi and somehow, someway, we had to help. He was, I knew, a compassionate man. But curiously, even before I arrived at the cabin, it was Garland who came rushing toward me.

"What?" I asked.

"It's Nellie. She's passed on."

Four

Guilt. Guilt. Guilt.
I had never regretted my behavior more than at that moment. Could I have saved Nellie if I'd been home? I'll never know. What I do know is that I promised to visit her. Instead, I ran off, behaving no better than a thoughtless child. I stared at the ground, hoping to avoid my husband's anger.

All that remained of Nellie, the mentor and friend who'd helped me adjust to living in a new place, were memories. I recalled how, when we arrived from Pennsylvania after our arduous trek through the Virginia mountains, she and her husband brought us a ham and a basket of wild grapes. Taking to us, they visited at least three times a week, advising how to make beans and corn grow in the hard Carolina clay as well as instructing us how to care for chickens and lure the wild swine inhabiting the area.

Nellie understood the earth and seasons. She also knew the Bible from front to back and fully embraced the message of

George Fox, the founder of the religious Society of Friends. She lived his teachings. In contrast to my skepticism, Nellie never wavered. Once I asked, "How can we Friends know we're right and everyone else is wrong?" Her lips turned up in a confident smile, and she closed her eyes. "My dear Mary Ruth, Friends were originally called, "Children of the Light," a good name for us, for all we're required to do is follow the light within our hearts. I cannot vouch for the light of another, only my own."

Not only had I failed to keep my promise to her, I'd voiced disapproval of her opinions during our last visit.

"Where were you?" Anger turned Garland's face red. A protruding vein in his neck throbbed. My soul actually shrunk so small, I considered lying to my husband. But when he touched me, lifting my chin, his clear blue eyes drained truth from my heart. My silence told him all he needed to know. "The orphan. You went to see the orphan," he accused.

"She needs us, Garland. Perhaps, we need her as well."

"Nellie needed you, Mary Ruth."

"Let's not speak of it now," I said, brushing tears away. "I must say good-bye to my friend."

"Other women are tending her. They prepared food; they bathed her."

Though I'd always thought I'd be the one there for Nellie when her time came, how could I protest? I'd let her down. All I could do now was visit, touching her sweet face one last time before they sealed her in the plain wooden box men had already prepared for her burial. Her final resting place would be beside her husband in the pristine cemetery located behind a row of elm trees. Recently, I'd braided her hair when she felt too poorly to do so. Perhaps the other women would allow me to perform that small service one last time.

When I entered Nellie's house, a half dozen women

turned toward me. "We were worried about you." said Cora Weaver. A hint of insincerity coated her tongue. Her thickly braided brown hair formed a halo about her horsey face. The stiff white apron she wore bore not one single stain or smear. When I asked permission to see Nellie, the brigade surrounding her bed slowly parted.

Dried herbs still hung from the rafters, scenting the room. Death had softened my friend's face, but a telling yellow hue still stained her skin. Her open eyes unsettled me. Reaching out, I closed them with my fingers.

"You'll need to place coins on them," Cora said, "else they'll open again."

I bent over Nellie, kissing her dry cheek. As I rose up, her right eye flew open, startling me.

Cora sighed. "Didn't I warn you?"

The body had been bathed. When no one objected to my braiding Nellie's hair, I found a brush and began by separating it into three sections. As I brushed and braided the silvery strands, I spoke softly, hoping by some miracle my words would reach her. "When my first child didn't survive, I wouldn't have survived without you. You were also there, Nellie, in the beginning, when Garland and I first arrived, possessing no knowledge at all of growing crops. You prepared a list, letting us know what would and would not grow. You were there again when I received the news of my own blessed mother's passing. And when I grew so sick with influenza after I lost a second baby, you bathed me and held my hand. Your herbs sweetened the stuffiness of our cabin; your soup warmed our bones on cold winter days."

I wanted to apologize, telling how I regretted failing to check on her, but I didn't. In the room, too many eyes watched; too many ears listened.

"Nellie left you a note," Martha Beeson said. "I was with

her at the end. She told me she loved you as if you were kin."

"And I, her." As I took the folded piece of paper. I feared that inside, written in Nellie's shaky hand, I'd find scalding accusations. Instead her message contained a simple message: Mary Ruth, follow your heart.

I frowned. I'd followed my heart, seeking out the orphan, but sadly, by doing so, I had neglected Nellie. My own stubbornness had taken over. Bowing my head, I prayed, "God forgive me." After my lips touched Nellie's forehead one last time, I left, letting those who'd been there when needed resume their somber preparations.

During out simple dinner of beans that evening, Garland, remaining silent, looked away from me. When finished eating, he stood to leave. Though I knew exactly what I must say, I had difficulty getting the words out. "I won't go across the river anymore," I promised my husband. "I won't seek out Naomi Wise ever again."

Though I bowed my head, hoping he would come to me, taking me in his arms, he didn't. Instead, his head held high, he walked outside without replying. After washing our plates, I settled the fire. When, finally, I took to the bed, I felt completely drained. For the next several days, I remained there. Heartsick that I hadn't the will to attend Nellie's funeral, I relinquished my fight allowing darkness to seep into my skin and bones. My heart ached. Like Nellie, would I also die? I wondered if Garland would even care.

I lived on broth and sassafras tea. After a few days, at Garland's insistence, I went outside to sit beneath the spreading limbs of the chestnut tree once more. There, grateful for a cool breeze despite the intense heat of July, I gazed at our property, remembering mornings when I could barely wait to be out-of-doors listening to the call of birds and watching sly squirrels pick up chestnuts in their paws before scurrying up trees, their plumed tails waving victoriously.

Forcing myself to stand, I walked slowly about the yard. During the six years since we moved from Pennsylvania, we'd transformed the lush wilderness into a useful productive farm. Though proud of our accomplishment, I still sometimes wondered what our lives would have been like if we'd never made that long trek from Pennsylvania.

I rarely mentioned to Garland how much I still missed my friends and family in the north. Before she died, letters from my mother had consoled me. Like me, she loved how words could connect people. Unlike my chicken scratch, her flowing penmanship described the world I'd left behind. When my sister Eudora welcomed a new baby, mother wrote, describing the pale hair and chubby cheeks of our newest family member. All the birthdays and holidays I missed were also lovingly described. But, alas, in her letters, she included the low points as well——the onset of my father's battle with cholera, ending in his death and the death of my brother Scott, her only son. Mother battled to hang on without them, helping Eudora with her children and later, taking in her sister Agnes, sick with ague. Both Aunt Agnes and mother died less than a month later.

Oh, how I yearned for my mother that afternoon. Going to the chest I kept at the foot of the bed, I kneeled to open it. Lifting the lid, I peered at items she'd given me: A necklace with a gold locket attached. Inside the locket was the pale brown curl she'd once cut from my hair. I lifted the tiny white christening gown she'd made with her own hands and sent before the birth of my first child. There were several letters from her as well. Picking up the one she sent after the loss of my first child, I unfolded it and read:

Oh, my dear Mary Ruth, what a blessing to have you as

my child. Even before the age of five, you helped me with household duties. Sometimes, you spoke to your brother and sister a bit harshly, but, I believe, they respected you for it. You provided a sterling example to them in regard to manners and accomplishment. You were meant to be a mother, my sweet girl. God created you to care for children and you will, I'm certain, do just that. I pray for the next issue from your womb to live and thrive. Nothing would please me more than to be a grandmother to your offspring.

Every day, I weep, missing you. Still, leaving with your husband was the right thing to do. Your life, there in far-off North Carolina, will be a bright star guiding others to be brave enough to venture out in search of freedom of worship.

The ending of her letter, Love forever, Mother, brought tears.

I never knew a more capable woman. Her dainty needlework decorated many items in my home, and I totally depended on her treasured recipes to charm others, fooling them into believing that I actually knew how to cook. Before I left, she'd warned me that living in a place without the friends I'd known most of my life would be difficult. "But I'm proud of you for sacrificing your comfort here for your beliefs and the beliefs of your husband," she told me. "God will surely bless you for it"

My mother, similar to Nellie, was all about love, loyalty, sacrifice, and forgiveness. Who would I turn to now that both of them were gone?

Unlike Mother, my father had strong opinions and possessed an independent streak I feared I'd inherited. An active man, he established a successful store in Philadelphia, selling all manner of merchandise shipped from across the sea. When not working, he loved to hunt, fish, and play cards of an evening, a bottle of brandy at his elbow.

There were times he bullied my sister Eudora and me, pitting us against one another. He did so, I believe, for the sport or it, meaning no harm. An industrious man, he provided well for us. Still he frightened me. When in his presence, I felt as if I were shrinking, becoming smaller and smaller. Now, in the presence of my husband, I felt almost as small and insignificant as I had with my father. Hadn't I been a capable partner for Garland, not only cooking, cleaning, washing clothes, but also working in the field and helping with the animals?

The next afternoon, after returning from the field, Garland sat in the chair beside my bed. "I've asked Arabelle to come stay with you." he said.

Arabelle was a former slave. She had escaped from a South Carolina plantation. Sometimes she helped Garland with plowing and tending crops. She lived not far from us in a one-room shanty with her two children. Three years before, her husband had been thrown from the back of a horse. Before finally succumbing, he lived six months with two broken legs.

At first, I stubbornly resisted any notion that I needed help. But on the day Arabelle came breezing through my door, I couldn't find it in me to turn her away. A tall thin woman, her skin was the rich brown of cinnamon; her body still bore scars from past beatings.

Frequently expressing her gratitude to me and Garland, she once again praised us for the protection we'd afforded her and her family. "To get to this place, we walked barefoot for over two hundred miles," she said. "When we be offered work by your kind husband, I went home and danced. Yes m'am, I did. I danced that night despite my tired feet, and sang songs sweet as a yellow bird to my poor hungry children."

Determined to make me well again, she prepared food the way she'd learned on the South Carolina plantation where she'd lived the first twenty-six years of her life. She often served rice with tiny chucks of dried apples tucked inside and goodly portions of collard greens. Another specialty was her catfish stew.

The following afternoon, while Garland was busy in the field, she rubbed the bottoms of my feet with foul smelling white powder, claiming it would cool my fever. It did. Later, she revealed the meaning of the tea leaves in the bottom of my cup. "I be seeing the end of your sadness, Ms. Eversole."

When I looked, all I saw were dark leaves, tiny as ants.

"What you need most is to spend time outside," she declared.

Because I longed to sit beneath the chestnut tree, I agreed to leave the bed, so with her help, I made my way down the stairs.

"You be getting your strength back soon enough," Arabelle declared as the two of us sat down near a field of drooping daisies."

Closing my eyes, I enjoyed the warmth of the sun.

"Before I'd had time to rest, Arabelle shouted, "Look up. There be your future."

Opening my eyes, I gazed where Arabelle pointed. "The sky, that's all I see."

See the clouds. That's where babies be floating. And they be heading right for you."

"There may not be another child for me, Arabelle. My first came early, never breathing a single breath."

"That was then; this be now." Her dark hand reached out, touching my stomach. She frowned, then closed her eyes and put her finger to her lip. After a few seconds, a radiant smile lit up her face. "New life already be stirring."

Overcome with anger, I screamed out, denouncing her for lying to me. When Garland, returning from the field, heard us, he ran to where we stood. "What?" he asked.

"Your woman, she be with child," Arabelle declared with a wide grin. "This one be coming into the world whole and lusty."

Her magic eventually weaved us into the spell. We stood there stunned. Suddenly, my husband's arms were around me. Pressing my face against his strong shoulder, I finally breathed freely and the dark cloud in my head evaporated. A child. A child. How my arms ached for a child to hold; how my breasts yearned to suckle a wee one. A child. A child. Perhaps, finally, it would actually be.

Five

Though memories of Naomi Wise never left me, I tucked thoughts of her plight in the bottom drawer of my mind. The top drawer remained crowded with thoughts of the infant I hoped to hold in my arms.

In our community, boys enjoyed an easier life with fewer restrictions and more promising futures, but nonetheless, I secretly yearned for a daughter, one with eyes as blue as Garland's. I imagined all we might do together. We could make quilts in the winter and pick berries in the summer. I would share memories of my beloved mother with her. As we cooked together, I'd reveal how to prepare the recipes passed down to me, including my grandmother's delectable rabbit stew.

Such thoughts brought both comfort and fear. Well aware of the perils of childhood, I knew that a large number of infants never made it to age two, particularly here in this rural place with no doctor nearby.

The prospect of having a child definitely cheered my husband. Suddenly, he walked taller. Sometimes, when he didn't realize I was nearby, he whistled a lullaby.

Right away, I wrote family members in Pennsylvania, letting them know that, God willing, I'd finally contribute to the family lineage. As I made plans for the birth, I imagined how pleased my mother would have been if only she were still living.

Though I had been shy during my first two pregnancies, I sought help from those in the community this time. Over the next few days, I noticed that the more questions I asked the women in my circle, the kinder they treated me. Martha Beeson, one of the older ladies, brought me rosemary. "Eat it crushed in warm cow's milk," she advised, "and it will surely cure morning sickness."

Arabelle did all the chores I requested and more. And as she worked, if I were nearby, she shared her thoughts on every blessed thing. One morning, as she dusted the bedroom, she took notice of the wash bowl and pitcher that had once belonged to my mother. Yellow flowers embossed the pieces. "Such a pretty thing," she said, touching the pitcher lightly with her fingers. "When your daughter marries, will it be passed along to her?"

I gripped my pillow and said nothing.

When Arabelle came to me, placing her warm sweet-smelling fingers on my forehead, I knew I must find a way to explain. "Though you mean well, I think we should speak of something else. This baby may not make it into the world, or like my two lost infants, this one could leave swiftly, mysteriously soon after arriving."

"Mr. Eversole warn me to be gentle, not allowing you to help out. But when I birthed my first one, back when I was still on the plantation, I picked cotton til the babe pained so bad I had to stop. Then I left off from the others, dragging myself past the big ole magnolia tree. Once there I hid behind a bush, just like my Mama tole me. When the sweet child drop out, I takes a knife and cut the cord. I did just that and I be proud of it."

"Oh, Arabelle, why did no one help you?"

"The cotton be coming in heavy. They couldn't leave the field. But my baby boy do just fine; I do just fine too. That what you needs to know. Tiny as babies be, they tough. When one dies it cause God takes back the sweetest ones to help him out in heaven."

Though I knew I could never deliver my own child, the knowledge that Arabelle possessed such knowledge was consoling. "I admire your strength," I told her. "Perhaps when the time comes you will help if the doctor doesn't arrive on time."

My words must have pleased her, for her face suddenly glowed and her thick lips opened in a smile so broad I saw she had a missing tooth. Pride must have straightened her spine as well, for that day she appeared even taller to me than her usual six feet.

After helping me sit up, she fluffed my pillow. "When your baby be coming, I be right by your bedside, making ever thing just right." Her confidence banished most of my doubts.

I noticed she limped when she came to my bed. Once when I'd asked about her uneven gait, she blamed the slave hunter who'd pursued her after she left the plantation. "He be a fat man; I be skin and bones, so I outlast him."

Placing one hand on my heart, the other on my stomach, she said "You be doing real good. The little girl inside you be doing good too." For a moment she paused, a serious expression banishing her smile. Placing her hands on her hips, she stepped close to me, whispering. "Listen now, and remember," she advised. "Know for yourself every detail bout what going to happen when you birth a baby. The not-know be what scare womenfolk."

A few days later, Arabelle suggested we go outside to eat despite summer's heat. "Folks need trees," she said. "There be nothing better for the spirit, excepting rain and moonlight. Folks need earth in their hands too, big handfuls of it to bring up to their face and smell. Few things be more healing."

I suggested that unhealthy bugs and worms might likely be crawling in garden soil. "No matter. Where you think folks come from? The earth, that where. And eventually that's where they goes back—to the earth. Earth be part of you, Mary Ruth, and part of me."

Once outside, I joined Arabelle with the celebration of the natural world. Elm trees spread their limbs as if welcoming us. The nests of wrens, tucked here and there among the branches, could be spotted despite a heavy growth of leaves.

Arabelle smiled as she kept her eyes on me, making sure I ate every bite of my hoecake as well as drinking a full glass of cow's milk. When I went inside to take a nap, she followed up the stairs and helped me into bed. While resting on my feather pillow, I allowed her to rub my swollen ankles, then lifting my dress, she sprinkled my stomach with pale brown powder while chanting words I didn't understand. "It keep the baby safe," she said, after completing her ministrations.

Against all reason, depending solely on intuition, I trusted this curious woman with dark smooth skin.

"Where your Bible be?" she asked. When I told her I kept it on a shelf in the main room, she went downstairs after it. "Good medicine in these pages," she said when she returned. Without asking permission, she sat in the chair beside my bed. "My people, least them that can, read the Bible. It be good hoodoo."

Though I'd heard the word hoodoo before, I wasn't quite certain what it meant. The puzzled expression on my face must have revealed my ignorance for Arabelle attempted to explain. "Hoodoo be good magic. My people, at least the darker ones, come from the Congo. They brought old beliefs and those old beliefs got all mixed in with new beliefs found in this place. The way God created the world in only seven days and give the breath of life to Adam and Eve, now that be almost the same as the hoodoo story. But some parts be different. God created Adam and Eve separate, not Eve from Adam's rib bone. See, in hoodoo, men and women, they be more equal. Moses parting the sea, now that be hoodoo. All them pretty Psalms in the Bible be hoodoo, too. Some of my people face the East when they read the holy book, hoping the words blow back protecting them in bad times."

During the brief time Arabelle had been with us, she'd changed me. She became someone I could relate to and even learn from. Still, in my heart, I harbored doubts. Those of us in the Friends community wrapped ourselves in the beliefs of George Fox. How could both we and Arabelle be right?

"If hoodoo is allied with Christianity, why do you use roots and spells?" I asked.

Arabelle's laughter, which seemed to bubble up from somewhere deep inside, filled the room. "Why hoodoo be that too." Her dark eyes gleamed. "I gonna find roots you need to protect you and a black cat bone to hold near your heart."

I shuddered. Did she plan to kill a cat to procure the necessary bone? "No, Arabelle, I wouldn't care for a cat bone."

"Any woman carrying a child always need to rub with a cat bone."

"No. Absolutely not."

"Then how bout a chicken bone." A great rush of laughter, free as the sound of a babbling brook, spilled out of her again. "Sometimes that be working too."

During those quiet weeks, as my belly continued to swell, both Garland and Arabelle agreed I should rest in bed after eating our big meal of the day. Never accustomed to lying in bed during the middle of the afternoon, I took to reading the Bible when I couldn't sleep. As I read the familiar stories, I thought again of Arabelle's definition of hoodoo and how magic could be applied to Noah's following God's instructions to save all the animals by building an ark. And as for Moses parting the Red Sea? That certainly couldn't have happened without something akin to hoodoo.

As I perused the book of Ruth, I discovered I'd underlined passages to read to Naomi. How was the child? I wondered. Closing my eyes, I recalled the last time we'd talked. But though I longed to see her again, making sure she was safe, I dared not leave the farm. The last time I'd done so, I'd been met with the grief of Nellie's death upon my return. I would never risk going to the other side of Deep River again, no matter how well planned and brief the excursion might be.

That evening, I was touched when Garland brought a wild rose to me. The next morning Arabelle showed up with incantations and, of all things, a clean chicken bone.

Determined to fight off lethargy, I took to snapping beans, shucking corn, and picking seeds from cotton bolls. Surely what I did with my hands wouldn't affect my unborn child. By August, because I'd had no adverse symptoms, Garland allowed me to pick blackberries with Arabelle. The two of us wore bonnets, protecting our faces from the sun. Arabelle brought along a tiny pot of pale yellow salve, which smelled even viler than the cow manure splattered here and there on the path leading through the woods. When we inhaled the sweet scent of berries, we stopped long enough to rub ointment on our ankles and wrists. She promised it would keep the agony of chiggers away, and so it did, at least from our wrists and ankles. But by the time we filled our pails with dark juicy berries, my swollen belly itched fiercely.

Though I began to think my Pennsylvania relatives had forgotten me, I finally received a letter from my cousin Nell. She wrote of the grand Independence Day Celebration she enjoyed with her husband Daniel Penn on July 4th. I thought of you as they raised our flag and rang bells here in Philadelphia, she revealed. Of all my cousins, you were the one who understood best the necessity of independence for our fledgling country.

I sighed, for July 4th had been my own birthday, yet no one in the community, not even Garland, had mentioned it. Sometimes the cost of striving to be simple and plain was almost too dear.

Going outside that afternoon, I sought shade beneath the chestnut tree, as I reread Cousin Nell's words again. At first I smiled, envisioning the excitement, but then thinking on how only a few actually benefited from independence here in America, my heart grew heavy. Though we were free of English rule, surely a grand accomplishment, tyranny abounded. I felt certain that the fear of what harm we might bring them had prompted the Indians, once inhabited the area, to leave. And what of Arabelle? At any moment, she might be discovered by a slave hunter. If caught, would she be beaten and returned to her owner or hanged? I did not know nor did I know what the fate of Naomi might be. Though fully aware that the government had declared all men to be free, what of the women?

A wild thought took hold of me. Would those of us considered the fairer and weaker sex ever be granted the right to vote and own property? I wondered if other women in the community shared such radical thoughts. Of course, if they did so, they, like me, would be too frightened to raise their voices in protest.

When Garland returned from behind our cabin, where he'd worked all morning, he surprised me with a sturdy chair of oak, the seat wide enough to accommodate my expanding girth. After kissing my cheek, he explained that he'd hoped to have it ready by my birthday, but with the crops requiring so much attention, he'd felt he couldn't devote time for woodwork.

"Oh, my Dear, in this life we've chosen, we have to do each day what has to be done, don't we? Besides, the chair would have been too large for me on July 4th. Now it's just right."

Later that afternoon, Arabelle arrived with tea which she claimed would help me sleep soundly and ensure the well-being of the child nesting in my womb. I said I would sample it later, yet doubted I ever would. I relied on familiar vegetables, fruits, and cow's milk for sustenance. Had my earlier pregnancies gone smoothly, perhaps I would have been more adventurous.

During our next meeting, the women in the Friends Society surprised me with a baby quilt, one they'd secretly worked on for weeks. Colors of black, rust, and brown formed the outline of a tree with birds perched on its branches. Nothing could have pleased me more. For our main meal of the day, Arabelle combined beans, rice, and slivers of hot pepper. For dessert, she served blackberries. Though tasty, each spoonful reminded me of the itchy chigger bites I'd endured.

Later in the afternoon, when the sun became less intense, I hobbled outside once more to the special chair Garland constructed for me. As I sat there, I placed the Bible on my lap. When it fell open to the Book of Ruth, I smiled as I recalled again explaining its meaning to Naomi.

Perhaps I could convince my husband to check on her. Maybe Arabelle could come up with a spell or find some root to protect the poor orphan.

Because Arabelle had cautioned me to keep my mind filled with happy thoughts, I closed my eyes to meditate. I heard the sound of jabbering jays and the call of a hawk. When I placed my hand on my stomach, I felt the baby move. Closing my eyes, I savored the sacred moment.

When I stood, the baby moved again. Then, a shrill sound floated up from down below, near the bottom of the hill, followed by a low moan, so pitiful I thought it would never end. Because I could not see who it might be, I ran toward the rough dirt road cutting across the back of our property. Pregnancy had made me clumsy. I knew I should slow down so I wouldn't fall, but I couldn't. I needed to get to the bottom as quickly as possible. Even before I saw her, bruised and broken, I suspected it would be Naomi.

Six

Sinking to the ground beside the orphan, I cradled her bloody head in my arms and pushed dark strands of sweat-drenched hair back from her face. Her right cheek was red and bruised. A gash, extending from ear to chin, bled and her right eye was swollen shut.

Taking the white cotton modesty piece from around my shoulders, I held the fabric tight against the wound, willing the bleeding to stop. Looking lower, I noticed that flog marks covered poor Naomi's thin arms and legs.

I screamed for my husband first, then Arabelle. Quickly they came, the expressions on their faces frozen by the horror of the scene. Gently Garland picked Naomi up, but she refused to let go of my hand, so the three of us walked together to the house. Once inside, I insisted she be placed on the bed Garland and I shared. Arabelle, spry as a rabbit, had run ahead of us and, as if by magic, already had needed supplies waiting. "I take care of her," she said. "Mrs. Eversole, you get yourself out of here and don't worry yourself."

Unwilling to leave Naomi, I pulled the one small chair in

the room closer to the bed. There I sat, holding the child's trembling hand as Arabelle ministered to her needs. First she bathed her. The water in the basin quickly became dark, filthy. Garland took it outside and returned with fresh water in the basin and a pitcher of it as well. He also poured a bit in a tin cup, which he held to the girl's cracked lips. She shook her head, letting us know she couldn't drink, but Arabelle, forcefully cradling Naomi's head, extended the cup again. "Girl, Git yer tongue wet," she ordered.

Garland insisted we use the ointments we kept to treat the girl's wounds. Placing her hands on her narrow hips, Arabelle proclaimed, "This be serious. She need hoodoo."

Garland shook his head. "Prayer. That's what this child needs." He stood straight, his blue eyes stern and his jaw lifted, as he willed us to bow our heads.

Later, while I stirred the potato soup already bubbling over the fire, my husband asked, "Who would do such a thing?"

Though I didn't know, I suspected the child's uncle and revealed as much. "We must let Naomi stay with us," I implored.

Garland placed his hands over his face, as if wishing no intrusion from his own thoughts. "She's not well enough to be moved now. I'll bring the matter up with the committee when we meet tomorrow evening. They need to be warned for their own safety."

"So, their words mean more than your own wife's? I want her here. That light inside of me, the one you profess to believe in, has let me know. From the first time I saw her, I knew she belonged with us. It would be good for me to have her close by, especially if this pregnancy becomes difficult."

"You already have Arabelle."

"You'll need her in the fields now that crops are coming

in."

"What will her people have to say, Mary Ruth? Have you even thought of the consequences? Those across the river are a dangerous lot."

"You have a gun," I said.

"Yes, a gun for hunting animals."

"It's still a weapon."

When his head drooped, I knew I'd won, at least temporarily. I intended to take care of Naomi until she was whole again. Then she could make her own decision, deciding where she would stay.

For the first two days, the poor child slept most of the time and when awake, she seldom spoke. The third day, Arabelle brought hoodoo medicine. Garland had already left for the field when she arrived, so perhaps he wouldn't find out. And even if he did, and the girl mended, how could he complain. The comforting tea and healing roots didn't annoy me, but how could I help but object when Arabelle, dressed in a long black dress, her head tied up in a colorful square of cloth, bought a pail of dirt she'd gathered from the graveyard.

I remained absolutely speechless as she sprinkled it in corners of the bedroom, then over Naomi's bruised body. Awaking, Naomi made a wild animal sound.

"Arabelle, I don't think this is a good idea," I protested.

"It be the way to protect her from demons."

"No demons are involved in this," I whispered to her. "I think it might have been her uncle."

"Then he be the demon. Anybody who done such be evil."

Finally, I convinced Arabelle that Garland needed her in the field and she left. Shaking the sheet covering the bed free of the dirt, I sat down. Naomi's hand found my own again. Intertwining her fingers between mine, she held on tight.

"I took a deep breath. Looking out the window to avoid

the hurt in her eyes, I quietly demanded. "You must tell me who did this to you."

When I looked back, both her eyes were closed. Suspecting she feigned sleep, I touched her shoulder. "Naomi, you will be safe here. Garland and I won't let anyone hurt you. But we need to know who did this, so we can warn others."

She groaned and opened her eyes. Then tears came, hers and my own. I took her in my arms. "Shh. It's going to be all right."

When finally she could talk, she said, "I tried to get away." When she looked down at her legs, she covered her mouth. A thin stream of blood extended to her ankle.

She was sweating profusely. Strands of hair, dark as a crow's wing, clung to her face. Anger twisted her parched lips. As petite as she'd been when I visited her, she now looked at least ten pounds thinner.

Filled with anger, I balled my fist, "So help me God, he'll never hurt you again," I said, then rose up, feeling so strong I temporarily forgot all that might go wrong with my pregnancy. Ignoring my own plight, I vowed to invest whatever strength and wisdom I possessed toward restoring Naomi. "I'm fixing you soup," I said, before leaving her side. "Potato soup like my mother made for me."

A week later, a perfect day finally came calling. The temperature hovered in the low 70's, neither too cold nor too warm. The peonies bloomed for the first time that year and wild roses embellished the fence surrounding our garden. Because the day was too grand not to be shared, I decided to bring Naomi outside. Arabelle agreed to help. Garland had already left for the field before I got out of bed, and soon as Arabelle assisted Naomi, she left as well. At first, the light startled the girl and she resisted, turning to go back. "Stay for just a bit," I urged.

For several minutes, my eyes absorbed the splendor of the pink and white roses that sweetened the yard. "Relax, Naomi. The fresh air will heal you." Inhaling deeply, I attempted to follow my own advice.

"Would you tell me the story of Naomi and Ruth again?"

I smiled, pleased. "Certainly." Hurrying back inside, I took up my Bible, all the while planning in my head how I could make the story more interesting this time.

That day was the turning point for Naomi. She laughed at a mocking bird and later at a squirrel, chasing its own tail. After reading to her and answering her questions about the passages, we sang "Barbara Allen" and "Lavender Blue." .

Though I smiled and offered encouragement, I had no idea what would actually become of her. The committee had advised Garland they could not condone his taking the orphan into our home. What if the uncle came after her, hurting others in the community? And even if the scoundrel never came, she still had no prospects. Without an education, how could she find work to support herself? Without a dowry, how could she ever hope to have a husband?

Despite that bright golden day, Naomi's prospects remained dismal as a swamp in dry season. But instead of dwelling on her future, I simply praised God for the smile lighting up the poor girl's face. The cut on her cheek appeared much better, and if Arabelle and her magic were to be believed, a hoodoo potion would make scarring minimal. Most heart-warming of all, Naomi had regained vision in her battered right eye.

I avoided telling Naomi the bitter truth that day. Though I disagreed with the committee's decision, I understood their reasoning. What if the Uncle and his kin came here shooting up the entire community? Such brutality was certainly conceivable. Friends were frequently taunted and belittled by outsiders. Indeed, most outsiders never called us Friends, the name we preferred. Instead, when they spoke of us, they called us Quakers and laughed, their way of poking fun, because sometimes, from the ecstasy of our beliefs, our bodies did actually shake. Some also used that word to describe us because they foolishly believed we were frightened of our own shadows. Unbeknownst to them, we were actually quite brave, but desiring to keep the peace prompted us to avoid fighting. Occasionally we'd hear of Friends being beaten for no reason except their simple beliefs. Sad tales had been reported of cruel men in northern cities cutting out the tongues of those in communities such as ours—Friends seeking to follow God's commandments for the sake of their own souls and to benefit the world.

Naomi reached out for my hand. Her skin felt warmer; she no longer trembled. "Whither thou goest, I will go," she said.

Yes, I answered, "and my people shall be thy people."

Bright sun blinked through tree leaves blessing our resolve.

Seven

During September, Arabelle continued her hoodoo incantations. When I reminded her of Garland's disapproval, she sniffed haughtily. "What do men approve?" Her insolence both annoyed and amused me.

She was, after all, no heretic, so why was it wrong for her to have beliefs considered odd by our standards? Weren't Friends, known to the world as Quakers, considered odd by those outside our community? The way Arabelle explained it, hoodoo was a combination of many beliefs and practices. Some of them had been brought from the Congo, the land of her ancestor's. Other practices, involving God as a conjurer, and certain passages of the Bible, labeled by some as magic or witchery, came from across the ocean. Additionally, hoodoo borrowed still other practices from Indians, the original inhabitants of the land where we now lived.

Wise and energetic, Arabelle became ingrained in our household. We could dismiss her, if we chose, but we couldn't change her any more than she could change Garland.

Actually, her beliefs resembled my own in some ways. Intuition provided her the insight to discern what might be going on inside a person. When she first came to help us out, she knew almost immediately that I was carrying a child. And wasn't the inner light we Friends claimed to possess only a step beyond, or perhaps even behind, intuition?

Of course, I never mentioned such wild notions to Garland.

Sometimes now, sitting here alone, practically everyone I loved dead, I wonder how much my silence eroded my marriage. Garland would have, I feel certain, been annoyed by many of my opinions. Though I tried to avoid shocking or embarrassing anyone, occasionally I voiced my inner thoughts to Arabelle or Naomi, carelessly letting them creep into casual conversations. How I wish my tongue could have been even more free and open then, as it is now. Expressing some of my scratchy thoughts to my husband might have saved us all.

By May, Garland took to carrying his gun with him at all times. Evidently, he believed that those living on the other side of Deep River might surprise us some afternoon or in the middle of the night, when the moon, flat as a hoecake, hung luminous in the sky. Though he was much admired for his contributions to family and community, he remained always such a quiet man. Only rarely did I venture to guess what might be on his mind. But during the first few weeks Naomi was with us, I knew something was eating on him. I smelled his uneasiness.

Naomi also changed by the end of August. As she healed, I recognized that she'd blossomed into a truly beautiful young woman, despite the small sickle-shaped scar just below her right eye. There, in the midst of Quaker women, striving to be plain, she, similar to Helen of Troy, celebrated in mythology as the fairest of the fair, caught every man's eye. Her dark hair shone as if touched by moonlight; her eyes, a rich brown, were fringed with long dark lashes, and the corners of her mouth turned up ever so slightly, enhancing her heart-shaped face. Though slender, she had a healthy look about her. In my mind, I took partial credit along with Arabelle, for the two of us made sure she drank plenty of milk and ate ample portions of butterbeans, squash, and greens as she continued her recovery.

I did worry about her, for now that she'd ripened, I detected something coy in her smile and in her eyes. I'd have to warn her not to use that look around men. It could easily be misinterpreted. In contrast, there also remained about her a childlike innocence that would have perplexed me had I not been familiar with her background.

Arabelle once commented to me that there were two Naomis. I smiled, understanding what she meant. Sometimes the orphan was quiet and dutiful. Other times, in a boisterous unbecoming manner, she shouted out when she spotted something in nature to admire; her enthusiasm often became as uncontrolled as water spilling over a rock. Once, when a bat flew toward her, Naomi chased the dark creature intent on catching it. When I explained that bats bit, and their bite had been known to sicken and kill, she ignored me. As she studied the creature's wings and head, she behaved as if she'd captured a rare specimen.

I warned her several times about picking up mice and snakes as well. But she longed to touch everything with her slender fingers—the fur of an animal, a flower, the wood of a chair, earth, water, as if, by touching, her fingers could absorb the essence of a thing.

Because she remained unwilling to give up most of the items she collected, I gave her a dented soup pot which she promptly filled with found objects, including a hawk's feather, a black snake skin, red berries, a crudely carved arrowhead, a silver button, a small rock, glittery with quartz, and mossy bark pulled from a tree.

I, too, changed as we grew accustomed to one another's ways.

Peacefulness settled over me. The companionship of Naomi and Arabelle buoyed my spirit, as I attempted to eradicate the scary memories of all that had gone wrong during my previous pregnancies.

Strangely, I took to activities I'd enjoyed as a young woman in Pennsylvania. I found a book of sonnets by Shakespeare, the English poet my mother admired. I read the musty book, letting each lyrical line drip into my psyche. I collected fallen rose petals, gathering them in a basket. I placed some of the dried lavender that had belonged to Nellie beneath my pillow at night, and as I inhaled its fragrance, I drifted off without a care, dreaming of babies. Fat babies, thin babies, blue-eyed babies, babies with eyes sharp as Arabelle's and hair as dark and silky as Naomi's. There were girl babies and boy babies, all cooing sweetly. During the remainder of August, this consoling dream visited practically every night.

With Naomi no longer confined to bed, I knew the committee would soon be discussing precisely what should be done with her. I appreciated that during the past two years women had been granted the right to have a say in some matters regarding our society. When I asked Garland to let me attend the meeting with him, he resisted at first, but later agreed.

"I'd also like Naomi to be there to speak for herself," I insisted.

I viewed a new Garland the day the committee met. Usually shy, he stood confidently before them, cordially smiling at one and all, as he proudly announced I was with child, which I'm sure everyone already knew. "Our two previous children didn't survive," he said. "Mary Ruth and I wish to do everything in our power to make sure this infant makes it safely into the world. Naomi is well now and strong. I've spoken to her about the possibility of staying on with us, at least until the baby's birth. She's agreed to take on most of the household chores as well as care for my wife if the committee deems such an arrangement suitable."

When asked about the threat of the Uncle, Naomi spoke up. "He's an old man, hardly able to walk." Though they appeared skeptical, she continued, "When I disobeyed him, he only whooped my legs with his cane. I guess I had it coming."

Garland and I looked at one another. How could her story be true? A cane wouldn't have gashed her face nor blackened her eye. Still most of those on the committee smiled, as if pleased with her watered-down version.

In my own plea, I spoke of Naomi's potential, mentioning her good nature and quick mind. "Eventually I intent to teach her to read," I said. "Though only twelve, she cleaned house and cooked for her uncle. We will expect the same from her. In return we will offer her a bed and a place at our table. As long as she's with us, I'll lead her spiritually by reading to her every day from the Bible. I also plan to teach her how to sew. Perhaps, later, that skill will make earning a livelihood possible for her."

When finished, they asked that we go outside while they considered our request. Somehow I endured the wait of over an hour, imagining all the while they would refuse us, but finally we were called back. Martha Beeson's husband Ben, who headed the committee, smiled congenially before announcing, "Naomi Wise may remain in the Eversole household, at least for now."

As we drove home in our buggy, I touched my husband's

arm. "Thank you, Garland," I said, "for supporting Naomi."

Naomi cleared her throat and dabbed at tears gathering in the corners of her eyes. "Mr. Eversole, when my mother died, I prayed to die as well, but now you and your wife have made me believe that my life might be worth something. I promise I won't disappoint you."

During the next three days, tranquility embraced our small farm. Though the sun shone every day, we had more than sufficient rain during the nights. The crops flourished, the cows mooed happily in the field and the pigs, obviously not realizing what fate would bring them during autumn, squealed as if delighted with their squalid existence.

The trees, bearing leaves of muted colors in September, awaited the brilliant full blaze of scarlet, gold, and mauve that would magically enchant the landscape by the end of October. Naomi, who now tended the herb garden, brought lavender, rosemary, and sage inside to dry. I praised her skill with the hens. The number of eggs produced almost doubled.

Despite the fortunate respite from trouble, some mornings an eerie foreboding overtook me, filling my spirit with dread. Once, when I ventured outside the house after dark, I imagined I heard a voice from behind the chestnut tree. Though I couldn't make out words, I believed it to be a warning, letting me know that feeling too contented might be folly. The next morning, as I made my way down the stairs and into the cooking area, Naomi brought me a bowl of mush. As she placed it in front of me, I realized something about her had changed. Finally, it dawned on me. The scar on her face had disappeared.

I must have stared a long while, for finally, she asked, "Mary Ruth, have I done something to displease you?"

"No, child, the mush is warm and you've never looked

prettier."

She curtsied before turning to leave.

"Wait," I said. Rising from my chair, I took her face in my hands and studied the place where she'd been cut. "Naomi, how could that horrible scar on your face simply vanish?"

Lowering her head, she blushed. "Arabelle took care of it."

"Ah," I said, beset by a flash of jealousy. Arabelle could help Naomi in a way that I could not. I hoped that whatever she'd done wouldn't hurt the girl later. The road ahead would be rough enough for Naomi without medical complications.

Even before dawn the next morning, a tall thin black boy, wearing no shoes and torn pants, banged at our door. "I be Arabelle's boy," he said when I answered. "She bad sick. Said tell you she ain't up to working no fields today."

Alarmed, I did my best to find out what Arabelle's sickness might be, but he didn't seem to know. When I gathered up a few things for her, including some soup to settle the stomach and, of course, dried lavender to sweeten her pillow, the young man appeared confused. I suppose my attempt to heal a healer shocked him. "Tell Arabelle to get word to us if there's anything we can do to help," I said, "and please keep us informed of her condition."

Soon as the boy left, running back into the woods, Naomi insisted on going to the field to help Garland. "Want me to gather the eggs first?" she asked.

"No, go ahead; I'll take care of the eggs."

At midmorning, as I meandered down the tiny path leading to the meadow where the hens gathered, an eerie sensation settled over me. Goosebumps rose up on my arms. Only a few times before had I experienced such a feeling of unease: once when I almost stepped on a copperhead, another time when a brown bear wandered into our backyard, bellowing loudly. And, more recently, when I viewed dear Nellie, silent and blue-lipped in her bed. I slowed my pace, examining my surroundings carefully, fully expecting impending doom.

After reaching the scattered hens, I felt more at ease. I called out to them, as I sprinkled their feed across the meadow. The haughty rooster, crowed, and stretched his neck, reminding me that I'd invaded his harem.

Strangely, the hens didn't rush for the food. They, too, appeared tentative, as if something was amiss.

After completing the chore quickly, I didn't pause, as was my usual habit, to determine the well-being of each hen. Instead I turned, anxious to get back to the house. After walking less than thirty paces, I discovered the reason for my unease. Weeds were flattened near the right side of the path. Splashes of red covered them. What awful thing had happened here? Reminded of the bloodiness when I'd lost my first child, I turned away. Why hadn't I noticed this spot as I walked toward the hens? Looking up the path a bit, I noticed a large boulder. Probably it blocked my view.

A fight between curiosity and fear battled within me. After a few seconds, curiosity won. Tiptoeing I followed the track of blood on the flattened weeds. Less than ten feet away, I spotted the victim, a man. His face was ruddy, giving me hope that he might be alive, but as I moved near, I recognized the same open-eyed gaze Nellie had worn after death. The lack of expression, except for a cold stare, clearly revealed he'd left the world behind. Of medium height, he wore a dark tattered coat and pants. By his side was a gun. The silver hilt of a knife extended from his neck.

In that moment, I placed my hands on my stomach, as if I could block the view from my unborn child. I knew I should touch the man, searching for a pulse, but I could not. The only response I could manage was a scream. Within minutes, Garland was there holding me in his arms, saying, "Shh, Shh." Naomi lagged only a few steps behind, her face pale as cotton.

Naomi spoke up, her voice flat, devoid of feeling. "It's my uncle," she said.

Since my husband and I had arrived, joining the Society of Friends here in North Carolina, there had been few disturbances. Now what would happen? Would this sacred ground be transformed into a site of disagreement, unsettling accusations and suspicions?

Finally, I understood the merit of keeping our distance from the rest of the world. Exposed to their ways, perhaps we'd become like them. This new insight caused me great pain, for hadn't I always been the one hoping for change, desiring adventure?

Never again, I vowed.

Turning, to avoid the gory vision, I felt a sudden impulse to look down. When I did so, I spotted a large four-leaf clover, lifting up, a deeper green than its siblings. After plucking the symbol of luck, I placed it in my pocket. Naomi stumbled toward me, her face streaked with tears. I took her in my arms. "He's gone now," I said. "He'll harm you no more."

"There are others, you know."

I took her hand, cold as well water and trembling. Smiling, I repeated words which I hoped would offer comfort. "My people are now your people. We will protect you; you have nothing to fear."

She managed a small smile, but Garland's face remained a mystery to me. Almost expressionless, he coolly discussed with us what must be done. "I'll stay here," he said. "You, two, go find Miles Jordan. Tell him what's happened and he'll bring others to help."

"How about the sheriff?" I asked. "Shouldn't he be

notified?"

"I'm sure Brother Jordan will look after every detail. After you explain where I am, go to the house, both of you. Bolt the doors. Mary Ruth, you know where to find my gun. Pry the floorboard open. Take it out; keep it by your side."

Fear nipped at my soul. Just do what Garland says, I decided. Follow his instructions and everything will soon be normal again. That awful day, I became an obedient wife, without a single desire to make any decisions on my own. For once, fear had me in a corner. What if I attempted thinking the situation through and came up with a bad decision that brought harm to my family or the community? Better to remain silent. Better to resist solutions. Garland, calm and logical, was the one to decide for us.

By the time we reached the house, Naomi seemed to have calmed down as well. I suppose that's why her question startled me. "Do you think your baby will be all right?" she asked as she made cups of sassafras tea for both of us. "Some people claim an unborn child can be marked by what the mother sees."

"Everything will be fine," I said, but suddenly I didn't know. Would any of us be all right again?

Garland didn't arrive home until late. Naomi served him lima beans which had been cooked early in the day. I had expected him to tell us all that had happened. Instead he ate in silence and soon after, offering no information except that the Sheriff had been informed, retired to bed.

Unable to sleep, I stayed up and so did Naomi. Lighting a lantern, I picked up the tattered Bible my mother had cherished and asked her to open it.

She looked down. "You know I don't know how to read."

"Now is as good a time as any to learn," I said.

When the Bible opened to the Book of Psalms, I read her

the comforting words of the twenty-third as I slowly placed my finger beneath each word: The Lord is my shepherd; I shall not want. He maketh me to lie down in green pastures: he leadeth me beside the still waters. Yea, though I walk through the valley of the shadow of death, I will fear no evil, for thou art with me...."

Then I read it again, explaining the sounds of certain letters. Together we must have read the passage more than ten times that evening. Naomi stumbled through, but eventually comprehended far better than I'd expected. As for myself, I found consolation in the words. By the time we'd completed the reading lesson, a sense of peace enveloped me. After I readied myself for bed, I prayed for sleep to restore me, helping me face another day.

Eight

Considerably renewed by the next morning, I awoke before everyone else. I placed new logs on the fire before placing slabs of ham from the springhouse into a pan already warming on fireplace ashes. Out of the pie safe, I took three of the eggs I'd boiled earlier in the week. Though usually our morning meal was mush, I felt we deserved something more substantial considering all we'd been through.

Who would see to the hens today? Perhaps Arabelle would be back. If so, I'd send her. Unlike me and Naomi, she had not viewed the dead body in the meadow, so gathering eggs there wouldn't be as disturbing to her.

The scent of food awakened Garland, but Naomi didn't stir. I decided to leave her be, at least for a while. Without her presence, I felt freer to discuss the day before.

Garland said not a word until he finished his first cup of coffee. Then touching my hand, he asked, "You all right?" The space between his eyebrows scrunched up as he examined me.

"I'm fine," I told him. "But I'll not go near the hens today. Perhaps never."

One side of his mouth turned up in a half grin. "Mary Ruth, I don't expect such of you. If Arabelle can't do it, I'll go when I return from the field."

One question hung heavy in the air. It had to be asked. "What was said yesterday when our neighbors and the sheriff showed up?"

After taking the last bite of ham on his plate, he lifted his hand to his right temple. His eyes were red, filled with pain.

"One of those awful headaches?" I asked.

He nodded.

"You're not alone. Except for me, everyone else in the house is unwell."

My husband, after breathing deeply, finally answered my question. "A great deal was said and gone over in our discussion, I'm afraid. The committee felt sure someone outside the community, probably someone in the man's family, killed Naomi's uncle. The sheriff believed just the opposite. He said it must have been someone here—one of the Friends."

"How could that be? We don't kill."

"The sheriff contends there would have been no reason for someone in Naomi's family to bother him. Does Naomi actually have any family besides the uncle? I'm sure those living across the river aren't afraid of us singly, but they're sure to know we'd band together."

"Yes, but isn't the idea of someone in our peaceful community inconceivable?"

"Mary Ruth, do we ever really know what vile thoughts

exist in another's mind?"

His answer chilled my bones.

Arabelle didn't show up until two days later. Naomi remained quiet and distant, but despite her malaise she managed to help with chores. Because she was afraid that if I went to see to the hens, I'd come upon another unsavory scene, which, in her opinion, might mark my unborn child, she dutifully saw to the loathsome chore. Once she returned, I set aside for another day all of the other chores except preparing our main meal.

Finally Arabelle returned to us. Though she appeared thin and drawn, she insisted on helping Garland in the field. How grateful I was, for his headaches still continued, making any movement pure drudgery. Though I volunteered to work in the fields as well, he objected, bluntly stating that my sole job was to protect our unborn child, bringing it to term. As he spoke his piece, I felt in my pocket for the dried up four-leaf clover, the one I had carefully wrapped in a lace-trimmed handkerchief, wishing for any luck it might bring.

That evening, dusty and tired, Garland and Arabelle returned to the house. Arabelle fixed a tea of roots, bark, herbs, and wild berries for Garland to drink. He declared it to be the foulest thing he'd ever had in his mouth, but by morning, he admitted his headache had finally let up.

My own spirit did not rally until the first day of October. By then the almost constant vision of the dead man that ran through my mind finally diminished somewhat. Moping was no longer an option. All of us had too much to do. Before the end of the month, we needed to harvest the corn, which would be needed to feed the animals during winter.

Within our community the conversation had subsided

somewhat over the continuing discussion of who might have killed Naomi's uncle. The committee decided to leave it to the sheriff to sort through. Still, they felt certain the guilty party, when found, would be someone from the other side of Deep River.

I was not so sure.

My intuition, surely a blessed gift from God, worked strangely. Sometimes, unexpected insights betrayed me; other times, the message sent was confusing. Still, I needed to be patient, trusting that eventually the meaning of thoughts pressuring my mind would become apparent.

One glorious afternoon, as I sat outside, awed by the glory of autumn, I drifted off. In my dream, Arabelle walked up to Naomi's uncle. "Leave the child alone," she warned him, her dark eyes flashing fire. "The nastiness you did to that orphan girl be clear to me. Stay away, else I send you to the other side." The uncle's large cavernous mouth, completely devoid of teeth, spewed forth vulgarities. Then he spit a stream of tobacco into Arabelle's face. "Get out," he shouted.

I awoke in a sweat. When I saw Naomi, returning from feeding the hens, I screamed out to her. She ran through fallen leaves of gold, scarlet and yellow to reach me.

"Mary Ruth, are you all right?"

I nodded to clear my head. "I think so. Still I would be most grateful if you'd stay nearby for a while."

Setting her bucket of eggs down, she sank to the ground near my feet. Looking up, she solemnly recited the twenty-third Psalm.

"The goal is to learn to read, Naomi," I reminded her, "not to memorize."

She blushed and then pointed to a blue bird delivering a wriggling worm to its nest.

Only seconds later the bird flew away again, seeking more

food for the new brood. A hawk, majestic and confident, circled overhead. Suddenly, the predator dived into the nest of squealing baby birds. Naomi turned aside, but I watched as the nest tipped over. Though she rushed to save them; she could not. The hawk was malicious and swift. In mere seconds, all that remained of the baby birds was a soft circle of feathers.

That afternoon, as Naomi and I stirred dirty clothes in the large black caldron filled with scalding water, curiosity got the better of me. "What do you make of Arabelle?" I asked.

"She can do anything. Get rid of warts. Rub pain from feet. Cure stomach aches."

"I agree she's quite amazing, but are you sure she's a good person?"

Naomi's mouth opened, as if she were startled by my asking such a thing. "She does good; that's what I know."

"This puzzles me, Naomi, if she's a real healer, why couldn't she heal herself?"

"Maybe it's only the body Arabelle heals. I think her illness had a different source."

"What then?"

"The spirit. Arabelle claims to get the down unders when she doesn't know what to do."

"Down unders?"

"Yes, sometimes she thinks she ought to be doing something to help, but she doesn't know what it should be. That makes her sad."

"Since coming upon the dead man, I've been plagued with the down unders myself."

Naomi smiled. "Life's like a bird in flight, ain't it? No telling if it'll go up or come down. No way of knowing at all."

"I suppose that's why I keep a four-leaf clover in my pocket. Does it really help? I don't know, but it's comforting to believe that somehow, someway luck might be obtained or earned."

Naomi's eyes lit up. Deciding she'd find a magic clover of her own, she searched through the grass. Giving up her quest in only a few minutes, she grabbed a low branch of a nearby tree and swung back and forth. Soon tired of the tree, she picked up a small rock, shiny with quartz. After examining it closely, she tucked it into her apron pocket.

How sad. Though still a child, she'd been forced by circumstances to be a woman. Calling out, I let her know I needed some help. The clothes I'd washed needed to be spread out on rocks to dry. Seemingly, without a care, she turned circles, gradually navigating toward me.

After our conversation, I put aside all misgivings about Arabelle. I couldn't fathom Naomi lying to me. If she believed Arabelle to be a good person, then so would I.

A few days later, I had another dream. The uncle, vile and despicable, was in this one as well. But when the vision of a woman's face, initially too foggy to identify, cleared, it was not Arabelle. Instead Naomi, appearing much younger and wild as a caged animal, was there. She screamed when her uncle lunged for her, grabbing her around the neck. She cried out, "Don't touch me. I'll tell, Mama."

"You ain't got no Maw. She's dead as a felled tree." He laughed crudely.

Naomi sobbed uncontrollably. Finally, the crying stopped. Crouched down, as if folded into herself, she stared up at him, her eyes cold, hard. "I wish you dead," she said, just before his fist came toward her face.

I awoke mumbling, "No, No,"

Garland shook me gently. "Calm down, Mary Ruth. Did you have a bad dream?"

I still had no idea what the Arabelle dream meant. Now another one, this time containing disturbing visions of Naomi. Getting out of bed, I stumbled to the wash bowl and pitcher and poured out enough cold water to splash my face. Perhaps the shock of it would drive away memories of my nightmare.

My mother believed dreams to be signals from God. As for myself, I resented the sprinkling of clues, with no definitive answers provided. Still I marveled at such night-time visions, and truth to tell, dreams often provided me with warnings. Though I never told Garland, I'd envisioned the fate of both our dead babies. I'd seen them cold, blue, and heard my sobs months before they were born.

I bowed my head in prayer. I can endure the recent nightmares of Arabelle and Naomi, but, please God, spare me visions of dead babies.

Thoughts of my Naomi dream lingered for more than a week, prompting a question I feared facing: Could Naomi have killed her Uncle? Could she, considering the injustice, have gained the strength to end his life? I didn't believe so, but perhaps she'd carried a knife in case he came after her. I could almost believe her plunging a knife into his neck to protect herself or to protect Garland and me.

Still, where had the knife come from? Though I didn't look at the dead man long, the etched hilt of the knife, extending from his neck, seemed familiar. Later I discounted the entire notion. I couldn't bring myself to believe that either Naomi or Arabelle could have committed such a heinous crime. But if not them, who might it have been?

   Despite occasional itchy suspicions concerning those two women, I became more and more dependent on them. The three of us became a team, determined to bring my unborn child safely into the world. Every day, Arabelle insisted I soak my feet in lavender water. Afterwards, she massaged my calves and ankles to keep them from swelling. Naomi made sure I sat down every afternoon by joining me near the chestnut tree. Soon, instead of my reading Biblical passages to her, she was reading them to me.

Nine

October soon became unseasonably warm. Without rain for nearly three weeks, the field became dry, unproductive. Garland, wishing to save the late crops worked tirelessly, gathering immature cabbages and corn. The corn would be taken to Dicks Grist Mill and ground up to feed our animals. Because all of us now detested going to the meadow to care for the chickens, he decided to build a small coop for them nearer our cabin. Though grateful, I worried that all the extra work would damage not only his own health but also Arabelle's and Naomi's .

One afternoon, Naomi returned from the field early. She complained of nausea. This wasn't the first time she'd spoken of an unsettled stomach. Before I'd believed it might be the tomatoes, seductively red and tasty, which she ate in abundance. When I warned that some considered love apples (as some called them) poisonous, she'd temporarily stopped eating them. After asking if she thought it might be something else she'd eaten or some herb Arabelle had given her, she turned from me, declaring "No, nothing such as that."

"What then?"

Without answering she stumbled back to the space where we cooked food over an open fire. I followed, asking if she'd like me to make soup for her.

"Please, no," she said.

When she sat in a chair, I noticed her protruding stomach. It frightened me mightily. What could it mean? The bellies of starving people protrude as did those with liver problems, but Naomi was young, her skin tawny and smooth. Perhaps some internal organs had been damaged when her uncle beat her.

I closed my eyes, determined to dismiss speculation. Going to her, I took her small hand into my own. Because her palm felt cool, I rubbed it vigorously. "Naomi, I think you need to see a doctor."

"Mary Ruth, I know what's wrong. Arabelle explained it to me."

"Then tell me."

"I can't. It would shame me for you to know."

How betrayed I felt. I fancied myself to be the closest person to her. Sometimes I viewed our relationship to be that of close friends. Other times, I treated her as I might treat a daughter. Why, then, would she share her secret with Arabelle and not with me?

Seeing the hard set of her jaw, I decided to let it rest, at least for the time being.

Rising from the straight-back chair, she walked out of the room as if in a trance. Though concerned for her, I busied myself with preparing food. Garland would surely be famished.

After cooking cabbage to go with the catfish my husband had caught early in the day, I walked outside to dip water from the bucket into the washbowl for Garland's bath. Startled by an unexpected noise, I turned, spotting two deer, both does, feeding on wild flowers. Obviously weakened by the lack of food and water, they were thin, their coats mangy. I couldn't bring myself to shoo them away. They reminded me of Naomi and Arabelle and their sad plights. Arabelle, smart and resourceful, had to hide from the outside world because her skin was a pale shade of brown instead of white. And Naomi was also shunned by many simply because she was an orphan. How could we ignore the message of the light by rejecting others, continuing to persecute them because of their color or situation?

I recalled Naomi's words: "I won't tell you what's wrong with me. I don't wish to shame you." This from a young girl who the community, including myself, had shamed with our suspicions and our pompous belief that we had the right to decide another's fate.

Garland walked up behind me, placing his hands on my shoulders. "It's good to be home," he said. "Arabelle and I needed Naomi today. The crops we didn't gather probably won't make it."

"Naomi's bad sick. We need to get her to a doctor."

When he said, "Damn," the word pained me. Garland rarely swore. Though I hoped he would apologize, he said nothing as he unlaced his boots and put them aside.

Peeved, I spoke words I knew he would resent. "If you don't take her to a doctor, then I will. She needs our help."

"I'm too exhausted to go tonight. We wouldn't find a doctor this late, anyway. It'll have to wait."

A while later, after my husband came back downstairs after washing up, I spooned vegetables onto a plate and handed it to him.

"Aren't you joining me?" he asked.

"I need to check on Naomi."

As I walked back to the small space where she slept, I sensed something amiss. Staring at where she'd been on a pallet, I called out her name. Maybe she'd gone to the privy, but, somehow, I knew I wouldn't find her there. I looked through her possessions. At first I thought she'd taken nothing with her, but then remembered the cracked cooking pot where she kept bird feathers, a button, a leaf, tree bark, and a small stone, among other treasures. I noticed it was gone. My Bible was also missing.

When I told Garland, he placed his head in his hands. When I saw his shoulders shake, I knew he must be weeping. Tears sprang to my eyes as well.

Surprised by his concern, I rubbed his shoulders. "Naomi's smart," I said, "fully capable of taking care of herself. It's already dark outside. We'll look for her tomorrow."

Pushing the plate of food aside, he rose from the table and headed straight to bed. Garland fell asleep before the full moon rose in the sky. He snored loudly, the sound resembling that of an injured animal.

Getting up the next morning, even before daybreak, I lit a candle and made tea.

With first light, I headed out to find Naomi. I looked in the barn and the privy, though I knew she'd be in neither place. I walked down to the river, looking over at the other side, wondering if she had gone there. As I walked back toward the cabin, I planned to go next to the henhouse, the place I most dreaded searching, but as I sloughed along, I spotted Arabelle standing by the well.

She hurried to me. "Mary Ruth, you sit yourself right down. In your condition, you shouldn't be stirring round so much."

"It's Naomi," I said, "I don't know where she is."

"She at my place. Showed up last night. Now she be sleeping like a lamb."

"She's sick, Arabelle. She said she told you what was wrong."

Arabelle smiled broadly. "That girl not sick; she be with child. I guessed it more than a month ago."

"She's barely thirteen."

"That be old enough."

"Who's the father?"

"She not say. But I figure it have to be the uncle."

"He's dead."

"She be at least three months gone. He be alive long enough to get it done."

Too stunned to know what to say, I sat speechless for the longest time. Yet everything surrounding me remained the same. Birds still chirped; squirrels still chased one another; fluffy clouds swam slowly across the sky, deciding whether or not to brew up a storm.

I didn't know what to think. I was still barely six months along myself. Going to my chair, I sank down, attempting to breathe deeply to calm my nerves. I knew the uncle's treatment of Naomi had been merciless, but I never considered rape. How could any man bring himself to force a child, especially his own kin? I needed to share the horrible news with Garland so that together we could decide what to do. One fact I knew for certain, I wasn't shamed by Naomi's pregnancy. How could I be? It was none of her doing.

Then another thought wiggled its way into my mind. If I found out she killed her uncle, I would even forgive her that.

Suddenly clouds completely covered the sun. Arabelle looked up, lifting her hands. Closing her eyes, she made humming noises and stomped her feet. A clap of thunder, then lightning streaked down hitting a tree. A huge limb cracked and fell only a few feet from where we stood. Finally, rain. A crescendo of water falling and falling.

Garland hurried toward us, shouting hallelujah. He lifted his face, allowing water to run through his hair and down his face. The three of us shouted and laughed. If we got a good soaking from the storm, and it looked as if we might, the remaining crops would survive.

Ten

Garland left to see to the animals. Thunder and lightning continued as Arabelle and me headed for the house.

Once inside, she stirred the flame in the fireplace and hung a small kettle of water for our tea, I cut corn from cobs to make soup and took dried apples from the pie safe.

As food cooked, I requested more information about Naomi.

Arabelle looked away from me. "She made me promise not to tell. That girl got a hot temper. She be savage as a clawing hawk when she find out you know."

"Why didn't she come to me?"

"Cause you be different from her. She ain't ever seen you do nothing wrong."

Stunned by her answer, I thought of Nellie and how I'd broken my word to her. I thought, too, of how often I'd disobeyed my husband. Too ashamed to admit my guilt, I protested, "But Naomi isn't responsible. How could she have resisted her uncle? We both know he beat her. Why I witnessed his neglect with my own eyes."

"She be worried bout what them Friends think. She be worried they convince you to send her away."

Arabelle handed me a cup of mint tea. The soothing scent settled me a bit, offering hope that somehow, we could get back to where we'd been before: three women helping my husband keep his farm; three women working together to grant safe passage to the infant within my womb. As I stirred the soup, a fresh idea came to mind. Later, in hindsight, I realized my plan was folly, but, at that moment, desperately wishing to protect Naomi, I convinced myself it just might work.

Wiping sweat from my brow, I took small steps to a nearby chair and sat down. "No one has to know about Naomi," I told Arabelle. "People in our church community rarely drop by anymore. They know we spend every minute trying to save our farm. Most of them, like us, are also struggling to care for their crops. Naomi only rarely attends Sunday meetings with us, so, if we are careful, we could keep anyone from seeing her."

Arabelle stuck out her lower lip. "Things always be found out." Her dark eyes pricked my conscience. Was the expression on her face anger or frustration? I wasn't sure.

"Just keep mum, Arabelle. Do that for me."

"Course I do anything you and Mr. Eversole tells me, but that not mean I think it be right."

When I hugged my strong honest friend, I wondered why it had never occurred to me to do so before. "I need your help. Don't talk about this to anyone else. I'll explain it to Naomi."

"What you be doing when Naomi's child come? You might

can hide her belly, but how you hide a squalling child?"

I never answered her question, for we heard Garland open the door. "Shh, now," I cautioned.

After the storm, Arabelle left to bring Naomi back to us. Hearing only a few remaining spatters of water on our tin roof, I walked outside. Sunlight drifted through trees. I turned to the right, hoping I'd soon be seeing Arabelle and Naomi heading up the path to the house. Instead I spotted a rainbow arc across the field. Closing my eyes, I inhaled deeply and silently thanked God for bestowing such a splendid moment.

When Garland finished eating, he joined me outside. "Smells good out here," I said, "like everything might be all right." Gazing into the depths of his blue eyes, I expected to see a man at peace with himself, but the storm cloud that brought us needed rain seemed to have settled within him. "What is it?"

He frowned. "Nothing." Then a tense smile curled the corners of his mouth up just enough to reveal a dark spot on the tooth just above the center of his lower lip.

Was he in pain? A rotten tooth could be pulled, thrown away. "How lucky we are," I told him. "The storm left our farm unharmed. Perhaps the smell of rain is the smell of victory."

Gradually the sky darkened again. In the distance, we heard thunder. Jagged lines of lighting cut through the sky.

"Don't fool yourself, Mary Ruth." My husband put his arm around my shoulders. "On this earth, there are no victories, only more battles."

I recalled the passage from the Book of Ruth—"Wither thou goest, I will go. Thy people shall be my people." I wondered how Naomi would respond when I told her, Thy child shall be my child.

Of course, no one would really believe the child to be

mine. The ages of our infants would be too close to make that humanly possible. I'd have to think of something believable—perhaps someone leaving the infant at our door or a cousin dying in childbirth, expecting me to raise her infant. That day, as much as I despised deception, I vowed to do whatever necessary to protect Naomi.

After Garland and I walked back inside, I again took up my needlework, a delicate christening gown trimmed with ivory lace. The previous week, I'd begun working on it.

Garland, exhausted, watched the progress of the storm out the window. As wind lashed limbs of trees about, I told him of Naomi's pregnancy. Curiously, he didn't appear to be surprised. "We must help her," I pleaded. "Her uncle raped her, I feel sure of that. How could she have stopped him?"

Massaging his temples with his fingers, he nodded agreement. "I can't imagine what her life might be like." He cleared his throat. When he didn't speak again, I looked up. When I spotted tears glistening in the corners of his eyes, my heart flew out to him.

He and I are alike that way, I believed in that moment. Both of us concerned for others, both of us wanting to lift whatever tribulations held Naomi back. As I voiced my proposal for altering the situation, Garland turned away from me.

"I suppose we must do something. We need her to help you and help with farm work. Sending her away would serve no purpose. Truly the other Friends in our community wouldn't wish us to abandon such a capable young woman."

The intensity of the rain made it impossible for Naomi and Arabelle to return that evening. How grateful I was to see their faces when they arrived the next morning. With no reservation, I hugged both of them, just as I would have hugged my sister if she had been there. After they ate, I asked Arabelle to go outside and help Garland chop up downed tree limbs.

Soon as the door closed behind her, I shared my plan with Naomi. She wasn't pleased. Before she even finished hearing me out, she flew into a rage. Moving back from me, she hit the wall with her fist. Clutching her stomach, she screamed. Finally, after a full minute of wailing, she faced me. "I've never before had a single thing to call my own, but this child is mine. I'll allow no one, not even you, to take it from me."

"We must keep your condition a secret if we are to harbor you from scorn."

"What does Mr. Eversole make of your idea?"

"It would be best for everyone, that's what we both believe."

When she sank to the floor, sobbing again, I rushed over, taking both her hands, now roughened by hard work, into mine. "It will be all right, Child."

Don't call me child," she screamed. "Soon I'll be a mother."

"Naomi, please listen. I never intended this to sound as if I'd take your baby from you. Soon enough, I'll have one of my own to tend. I simply thought, for the sake of everyone, it might be best to keep it quiet."

Reluctantly, she agreed, but let me know that after the child was born and she was well enough to leave, she would. "Always there's been someone telling me what to do," she said. Perhaps that's why everything sours."

"Know that I'll do whatever I can to help." Bending toward her, I pushed back the wet stringy hair covering her eyes and kissed her cheek.

The tensions within the house eased up during the next month. Rainfall increased during November and Garland caught and slaughtered three large swine. I offered up many prayers of gratitude, not only for the plentiful rainfall and the meat we'd have for winter, but also for my husband who tolerated the constant company of women.

I will always wonder if the sickness, afflicting Naomi early in her pregnancy, didn't result from a guilty conscience, for as soon as I learned of her delicate condition, her nausea and weakness abated. Of course, Arabelle took credit, claiming the mixture of herbs and roots she provided had hastened the cure.

Before I lost my first child, Garland crafted a lovely cradle of oak, carving heart shapes into the wood and attaching rockers to the bottom so I could gently sway our baby back and forth. That child died before I could use it even once, so I saved it for the second one, who spent only a brief time on this earth. Unable to bear seeing this reminder of my dead children, I gave the cradle to Naomi for the baby she expected. Garland promised to build a new one for our expected child. I begged him to make it less ornate than the one I'd given to Naomi. My heart kept reminding me to follow the Quaker path and keep things plain.

Each afternoon, Arabelle still rubbed my ankles to prevent swelling and insisted I drink root tea before she left for her rustic shack in the woods.

Though I continued to wonder if all the attention I received did more harm than good, how could I object when everyone insisted that rest would be best for the baby? Reluctantly, I submitted to letting Naomi prepare the meals and do most of the chores. Sometimes, when the weather wasn't too wet or windy, I went outside, but by the end of November I was spending most of the time in bed.

Staying busy appeared to make Naomi happy. And the more advanced her pregnancy became, the more energy she seemed to possess. Often she sang ditties as she worked. My own state was one of unease. Though I still loved Naomi as if she were my own kin, I felt the bond between us loosening.

Eleven

The visions of leaves shivering on trees brought to mind the winter parties I'd enjoyed before I left Pennsylvania. Ladies dressed in glorious gowns would take off their wraps when they arrived, even when snow covered the ground outside. How beautiful we were. Yes, how beautiful and cold. There would be talk and laughter among the young men as we, the young women, waited to be asked to dance.

One night, when my Aunt Regina and Uncle Bartram entertained, Garland showed up. How fine he looked. Standing tall, he glanced at me from across the room. Even before he asked me to dance, I fancied he would be the one I'd marry.

Still I never once imagined how difficult our life would be. I suppose if young people in love could gaze into the future, there would no longer be weddings or babies.

Still, why should I complain? We had stored away plenty of food for the winter. Our livestock remained healthy and fruitful. According to Arabelle, who once a day placed her hand on my ballooning stomach to check the movement, the babe would arrive by the next full moon.

"Will my child be healthy?" I asked.

"Your child will be whatever she be intended to be."

"So, you think I'll have a girl."

"It surely be so."

"How do you know?"

While you sleep I hold a button tied to a string above your belly. It move side to side. If you be having a boy, it would move up and down."

Should I put my faith in Arabelle's words? I wasn't sure, but I chose not to question her predictions. Soon enough, God willing, I'd be holding the evidence in my arms.

Throughout my laying in, I dreamed of my baby. Earlier on, I dreamed of many of them, both rowdy boys and serene girls, but during the final month I dreamed of only one child, always a girl, just as Arabelle predicted. She was blessed with her father's curly blond hair and eyes as blue as the sky on clear days. Hopefully, she would also inherit his usually even personality. That would make her life easier. Still, if her moods, like my own, sometimes romped here and there, I silently vowed to help guide her from the sorts of mistakes I'd made.

Suddenly, in the middle of the month, a bubble of excitement took over. Though I tried to follow all Arabelle's instructions, even consuming the bitter tasting root tea she prepared, the beauty of autumn leaves often lured me outside. "I'll wrap up; I'll rest out there," I promised.

Arabelle fretted and scolded anyway. "Master Eversole, he want you to be careful," she said at least a dozen times a day.

Though Naomi claimed she'd never felt better, Arabelle fussed over her as well, insisting she drink at least two glasses of cow's milk each day. "She be too young to have a young one," Arabelle once said to me. "Naomi's bones not be hardened up yet."

Labor began Thanksgiving Eve. I woke up next to my husband, who was still sleeping with his right arm around me. I decided not to wake him. At least not yet. Getting up, I cautiously made my way across the creaking floorboards and down the stairs to the main room. By the time I'd made tea, the pains increased in intensity. The distance between the pains quickly decreased. I soon heard Garland stirring around upstairs. Within minutes he joined me, kissing the top of my head. "Is it time?" he asked.

"Finally."

We smiled at one another, grateful for a quiet moment together. "I'll go after the doctor."

"Stay," I said. "By the time a doctor gets here, I'll be holding the child in my arms. But do let Arabelle know."

"I suppose both of us sensed that something might go wrong, and this baby might join its siblings, so he hesitated a while longer. Before he left, Naomi joined us. Holding my hand, she assured me that all would go well. "God rewards good women," she said.

"Oh, Naomi, I no longer believe in rewards. What happens to us is willy-nilly, pure chance it seems."

Later, after making sure I was reasonably comfortable, she left to feed the chickens. When she returned, she grinned broadly. "I found something for you," she said.

Perhaps a pretty stone or a bird feather, I thought. Naomi was forever looking at the ground, searching for objects to add to her collection. But it was neither. In my palm, she placed a tiny four-leaf clover. "I found you luck," she said.

"How did it possibly survive the cold?"

Neither of us had an answer.

By the time Garland returned with Arabelle, Naomi had warmed water over the fireplace and stacked clean cloths, ready and waiting, on a straight back chair. Arabelle held my wrist, while she instructed Naomi to go to the bedroom and put a clean sheet on the bed. Then she turned to Garland, asking him to go outside and wash the cradle he'd made for our baby. When he returned, he tenderly lifted me, as if I were a fragile object, and carried me up the stairs.

"It gone be quite some time," Arabelle warned him. "Get yourself outside and keep busy. I send for you the minute the baby be here."

How relieved I was that he didn't argue with Arabelle's instructions. The walls of our cabin had absorbed too much disagreement. Maybe with the birth of my child, the negativity would diminish.

Standing over me, he lifted my cold fingers to his lips and kissed them before leaving.

Soon as Garland walked out, shutting the door, Arabelle issued orders to Naomi. "This gonna be quick. Go get hot water and them cloths we prepared. But first, pour a bit of the brandy Mr. Eversole keep for medicinal purposes into a cup." Pausing, she squinted her eyes and pursed her lips. With hands on her hips, she scolded Naomi. "I be depending on you, girl. You needs to be quick. Don't you be letting Mary Ruth down."

Naomi's face paled. She hurried down the steps. By the time she returned, the baby had already crowned.

I'm sure I must have been in a great deal of pain that morning, but I have no memory of it. All I recall is a joyful buoyancy. And I recall, too, the moment Arabelle placed my cleaned-up daughter in my arms. I examined everything about her, even looking in her ears and up her nose, and then counted her fingers and toes, making sure none were missing.

"She's perfect," I said, "Absolutely perfect."

"Her color good. She be a nice size. I spect she weight seven pound or thereabout."

When Garland first saw his daughter, he smiled broadly. My eyes misted and so did Naomi's.

By the next morning, all the joy I'd felt the day before flitted away. Anxiety, worrisome as a wasp, crept in. I constantly worried that the baby was sleeping too long or that her breathing was too slow.

Arabelle scolded, "You gots to stay calm for your child's sake. Else your milk won't come down."

But even that never posed a problem, for by evening, my swollen breasts were sticky with milk and when Arabelle handed me my daughter, she suckled like a greedy pig.

"What you and Mr. Eversole gonna name this split-tail?" Arabelle grinned.

"We haven't decided."

"You had nine months to think on it."

"Oh, Arabelle. We were never even certain it would be."

Sighing, she turned from me and busied herself straightening the room.

The next morning, I bought up the matter of a name for our daughter. Garland suggested we name her for her two grandmothers. Cornelia after mine; Viola for his.

To my ear, Cornelia Viola sounded awkward and much too formal. Besides, though I didn't voice my concern, I didn't take to the idea of naming our daughter for two dead women, no matter how dear to us they might have been.

"Tell me what you're thinking?"

"I'd like to name her Belle," to honor Arabelle. "I credit

her with making it possible for me to carry this baby to term."

Garland's face sagged in disapproval. I understood his concern. Still I wasn't going to relent. Arabelle had become much more to us than hired help.

After thinking on it, he finally relented, "You've given me a beautiful daughter. How can I deny you anything?" Taking our baby from the cradle, he held her close and looked down at her angelic face. "Your Mama insists on naming you Belle, so that's who you'll be, our beautiful Belle."

We soon slipped into a routine. Garland graciously allowed me to still have Arabelle with me. I needed her for all the chores she managed, but even more for the reassurance her presence provided.

Our precious Belle, with her plump huggable body and yellow curls, reminded me of pictures I've seen of cherubs. I couldn't get enough of feeding her, tending her. I actually fought pangs of jealousy when either Arabelle or Naomi held her in their arms.

Garland treated Belle if she were a miracle that might disappear if we weren't careful. "Don't hug her so tight," he once cautioned me. "You might hurt her."

Later I would regret laughing at his caution.

Six weeks after Belle's birth, the sound of tree branches, scratching against the window, woke me. It was still dark outside. Garland slept soundly. One of the benefits of being a farmer is that after laboring so hard through the day, sleep comes easily at night. Keeping as quiet as possible, I got out of bed to check on the baby. In the dark, I stumbled to her cradle, the one Garland had so lovingly made for her. Bending down, I moaned, for I still suffered a lingering pain or two from her birth. Carefully picking her up, I held her against my heart, waiting for her to wiggle, listening for the soft sound of her exhalations. She felt so heavy.

"Garland." I screamed, "Wake up. Light a candle." I suppose I already knew and Garland surely heard the sad knowing in my voice, for, without hesitating, he came.

When he held the lit candle above Belle's head, we saw what we already knew. The infant we'd wanted so desperately had been snatched from us. Her lips were already blue.

Garland tried taking the baby from me, but I wouldn't let go. Sinking to the floor, I keened as I held her dead body. I heard Naomi's feet on the stairs. Without a single word, she came to me, holding me as gently as I held the baby. Garland, stunned and speechless, still dutifully stood there clinging to the candle.

My mind must have flown off someplace else. With no tears left inside me, I lifted my daughter's tiny hands. "See," I said, "ten fingers." Then cradling her precious feet in my hand, I said, "Ten toes. I closed my eyes briefly. Opening them, I smiled. "See, a perfect baby. "Nothing's wrong," I screamed. "Absolutely nothing!"

A good Quaker strives to remain reasonable and sane. Following the death of my third child, I ignored such expectations. Letting go of all inhibitions, I became totally unreasonable, totally mad. At first, I refused to consider a burial, demanding the child be left with me. Naomi couldn't reason with me, and even Arabelle, attempting to force me to eat roots to ease my grief, made no impact. Indeed, an enormous mistrust of Arabelle grew in my heart. She'd told us how to care for the baby. She'd told me what to eat and what to avoid before the child was born. Perhaps her advice had caused my daughter's death.

Garland became practically mute, only speaking

when absolutely necessary. Neighbors came, whispering consolations, offering to tend our crops and livestock. Arabelle led them to the fields and barn, explaining what needed to be done.

I barred the bedroom door, refusing to let anyone come inside. No one was to see Belle. Only Naomi was allowed to stay with me, for despite the madness that crushed my spirit, I wanted my daughter protected from prying eyes.

The third day after my baby left us, Naomi brought me something to eat. Huddled in the bedroom, I'd placed several sprigs of lavender in my daughter's crib, but the sweetly scented herb did little to soften the smell of death. If it had not been a bitter cold November that year, the stench would have been intolerable.

When Naomi held the plate of beans and rice in front of me, I turned away. "I'm not hungry," I whispered. How could I be?

Before, everyone had been sympathetic, letting me have my way. I suppose I must have been insane enough to expect such treatment to continue, but Naomi, her eyes fierce and her mouth protruding in a pout, was having none of it. "Stop it," she yelled. "This is no time to think only of yourself and what you want. Think of your husband. Think of your baby." Then, hurrying to the crib, she picked up the remains of my child, wrapped tightly in a blanket and handed it to me. "Give me permission to tell Mr. Eversole his child will finally be buried."

If it had been anyone else, I wouldn't have listened. When finally able to speak, my voice sounded rough and low, more the voice of a wild animal than a human being. "Please don't let them put Belle in a coffin. Make sure she's buried in her crib."

"I'll tell them." Then, taking the baby from me and

returning her to the crib, she led me downstairs.

Garland constructed a wooden covering for the baby's crib and buried her down close to where wild roses would bloom the following spring. Most of the Friends in our community came, bringing food and offering prayers. Naomi, bless her heart, remained hidden for two days in the shanty Garland had recently built to protect the hens from storms. And Arabelle, aware of the foolish accusations I'd made about her, stayed away. During the short service, one of the Friends read the twenty-third psalm. More appropriately, I believed, would be the passage from Ruth: "Whither thou goest, I will go," for during that time, at that place, I wanted nothing more passionately than to follow my dear sweet Belle to the grave.

Twelve

Making it through the next week was near impossible. My arms ached for my lost daughter. I felt neither hunger nor thirst and sleep deserted me. Though my husband offered comfort, I turned from him, for in the sadness of his eyes I witnessed the reflection of my own grief.

Eventually, my mind led me to recklessness. Desiring to feel something, anything, I went to the river, stripped off my clothes and jumped in. I wasn't cold, for I was beyond all sensations we take for granted. I no longer experienced cold or hot, hard or soft. Grief robbed me of all sensitivity.

I heard Naomi call out "Ruthie" before I saw her. Almost immediately, she stood in the stream beside me, lifting my head above the water line. Finally coaxing me to the shore, she helped me dress.

Though I expected her to scold, perhaps even tell Garland, she did not. Instead she admitted that once, when she'd lived on the opposite side of the river, she attempted a similar act of desperation. "Everything felt so heavy then." she said.

"I believed river water would help wash away my sadness. Perhaps it will do the same for you."

"Naomi, you saved me." I took her hand, letting it warm my own. "Back when you had troubles, who saved you?"

"I saved myself. There was no one else."

The next day, hidden near the back of the woodpile, I found the home brew my husband kept for medicinal purposes and drained the jug dry. I despised the fuzziness that lingered in my head, but the resulting release of constant thoughts of death made it possible for me to sleep until noon the next day. When finally I awoke, I walked to the river where I floated leaves. I watched, intrigued, as the water carried them away.

During the next week, I ate sugar, teaspoons of it at the time, hoping it would sweeten the sourness overtaking me. When I took to scooping up red clay to eat, revulsion swept over me. Once Naomi walked nearby as I licked red mud from my fingers. "Are you sure earth is what you crave?" she asked.

Days crept by—slowly, sadly.

I informed Arabelle her services would no longer be needed. Without protest, she prepared to leave. "If Naomi have pains, you come for me, she said before walking out the door. "Tell Mr. Eversole there be no charge for that."

"It will be at least a month," I said, as if I'd become an expert concerning such matters.

"With birthing babies, it hard to know exactly when," she said as she left, carrying her bundled up magic tied up in a bright piece of green and blue cloth on top of her head.

Though briefly tempted to hug her as I'd done after the birth of Belle, I turned away.

That evening, feeling alone and betrayed, I tried to meditate as I sat listening to the hiss of the fire, but my mind remained shattered as a broken dish. Then the awful truth became clear to me. I liked having Arabelle to blame for my child's death. I found it far more tolerable than blaming myself.

Blaming God as well, I insisted we keep Christmas small—no berries, no pine boughs, no lighting of candles, no singing. Garland attended service at the meeting house, but I never left the bedroom the entire day. Once I had loved snow, but when I glanced out the window, beholding a few flurries, more grief than I could bear rolled over me. Swallowed up by sadness, I could neither cry nor speak.

Nothing pleased me that long dark day. I wondered if anything ever would.

After the New Year began, I dedicated myself to helping Naomi prepare for the birth of her child. Staying busy helped me avoid the grasp of sorrow during daylight, but every night bad dreams returned. I envisioned men dying in battle, women dying of pox and babies turning blue before they uttered a single whimper.

Naomi asked me many questions about babies and giving birth. I was never sure if she really knew so little or simply used the ploy, hoping to keep my mind occupied.

I gently described to her the discomfort of labor contrasted with the exhilaration of holding a child of your own in your arms. I cried as I handed her the clothes I'd made for Belle. "What do you wish for?" I asked. "Boy or a girl?"

At first, she didn't answer, even turned away.

"Well," I said, "what is it?"

"It doesn't matter. I just want to do right by my baby. I genuinely do."

I patted her hand. "Of course you do and you will."

Unlike my daughter, born during the night, Naomi's son make his appearance in broad daylight, less than a month later. Badly as I'd treated her, Arabelle dutifully returned without complaint for the delivery. Though I'd offered to be there assisting her, she shooed me out of the house.

Garland and I were both shocked when called only a short time later. Arabelle held the infant in her arms. "A blessed boy," she said.

When I pushed back the blanket covering his face, I squealed. Frail and scrawny, the tiny face and arms were wrinkled. As much as anything, the unfortunate child resembled a miniature old man. Arabelle guessed his weight to be less than five pounds.

"You be the one to tend him," she ordered me. "Naomi be too young for birthing. It gonna take her time to recover."

Before I could protest, she plopped the small bundle in my arms. "He be yours for a while," she said, giving me a hard look, signaling I'd best offer no complaints. "Mind that you do right by him."

Before returning upstairs to the bedroom, she let us know she'd stay with Naomi until nightfall, then return to check on her and the baby the next morning.

Why should I have to look after Naomi's baby? I was still emotionally drained, an empty vessel grieving the loss of my own child. Yet, despite all the objections wheeling through my mind, I felt milk miraculously flow into my breasts again. How could that be, I wondered. But, later, when I tried explaining to Arabelle, she grinned broadly. "You must of willed it. Willing something be powerful medicine."

Though I resolved to do what I could to tend the wee one, I vowed, as well, to keep my heart locked up. Oh, I felt pity, but I wouldn't allow myself to love the baby boy. His chances for survival didn't look good. Even if he lived, he belonged to Naomi, not me.

Late afternoon, before leaving to return home, Arabelle examined every inch of the babe, all the while nodding her head. She instructed me to let him suckle, but warned he might be too weak to do so. "If he can't, put milk on your pinky finger, then stick it in his mouth, rubbing it against his cheeks and tongue."

Despite the fear I'd be rejected, the baby latched onto my breast, but nursed less than a minute before nodding off. Putting him in his cradle, I bent near to hear his breathing. Naomi, agitated and disoriented, opened her eyes. "Is my baby alive?" she asked.

"The baby's fine, dear," I answered. "Go back to sleep. Arabelle says you need plenty of rest."

"Will you take care of him for me?"

"I'll do my best," I promised, "until you're well."

The next day, when Arabelle arrived shortly after daylight, I had the infant at my breast again. He nursed longer than the day before, yet still remained too weak to consume much nourishment. After she examined him, she touched my cheek. "You did good. His color look better; his breathing sound fine. God willing, he just might make it."

Our voices must have awakened Naomi. She looked toward us. "Would you like to hold your baby?" I asked. Without waiting for an answer, I carried him to her. "Here's your, Mama."

He squirmed and frowned. When Naomi looked him over, I recalled how I'd examined every part of my own child during the brief sojourn she'd been with me. I recalled how obsessed I'd been with her ten tiny fingers and toes.

Naomi's eyes filled with tears. "What's wrong with him?" she asked.

Arabelle spoke softly, a rarity. "He be born nearly two

months early. He small, that all. Otherwise he appear healthy."

"Will he live?" Naomi's voice was flat, distant.

"Babies don't come with guarantees," Arabelle answered.

I expected Naomi to be more upset. I knew I would have been if he were mine. Instead, she turned over, promptly returning to the safety of sleep.

Over the next few weeks my new task proved a blessing, for on Naomi's baby, I could pour out the attention I'd desperately longed to give my own daughters, all three now in a heaven I couldn't visualize. I loved touching his warm skin and inhaling his milky breath. Still being near him was fearful, for I knew that Naomi would eventually want him back. Though with all my heart, I wanted her to take her own sweet boy into her arms, I couldn't imagine him ever leaving mine.

The thought of sharing my thoughts with Garland caused me to quiver inside, closing up my throat so I could barely speak, but, somehow, one afternoon, when he returned from the field, sweaty and exhausted, I managed to relay to him all he needed to know.

His grin surprised me. He took the child from my arms. Calling him David, he lifted him up, as easily as if he'd been practicing. "I'll teach you to farm," he said, "and ride a horse."

The infant opened his eyes, as if comprehending every word.

Making sure my husband understood, I again went over all Arabelle said, letting him know that having the baby with us was temporary. "Later, Naomi will surely demand her own child. She may even move from here."

Garland, still holding the tiny boy in his arms, looked both earnest and proud. "Everything's temporary, Mary Ruth.

Absolutely everything. Nothing stays the same."

The baby whimpered.

Getting up out of my chair, I walked to my husband. The sweet tug of milk flowing into my breast provided me with confidence I'd never possessed before. I took my temporary child from him. Sinking back into the rocking chair, I exposed my swollen breast. My husband stood there for the longest while, a look of awe on his face, watching me nurse Naomi's son.

By the middle of December, Naomi was up and about again. Still she resisted tending to her son. Instead she took over many of the household duties, including cooking and cleaning. Though more than satisfied with the arrangement, my heart tugged for her, so I rarely failed to offer her a chance to rock the baby asleep and put him in his crib, but she usually offered some excuse. Eggs needed to be gathered, she'd tell me. Or the goats Garland recently purchased needed to be fed.

Arabelle continued to check on the baby, assuring me that whatever I'd been doing must be right. She estimated his weight had increased by at least three pounds. He already slept through the night, quite extraordinary for a two-month-old infant. During the day, as he slept, I cut out and stitched clothes for him. Most were made from Garland's discarded shirts. Because the soft gowns I'd had for my own babies was a reminder of the daughters I never had a chance to know, I rarely dressed Naomi's son in them.

One evening Garland announced, "We'll be celebrating the Christmas we avoided this coming Sunday. Since Davey joined our family, our sorrow has been replaced with joy."

On Saturday, he cut down a fir tree. The fragrant scent of it filled our house. Naomi was in her element as she searched outside for pinecones, empty bird's nests, and bright red berries for decorations. Proclaiming herself Sister Christmas, she wound red ribbon through her hair and tied a cow bell around her neck.

Garland killed our biggest hen which I placed in the big black pot hanging over the fireplace. I added potatoes, an onion and herbs. Though Arabelle let us know her beliefs didn't include celebrating cause she and her family never had money for such, I enticed her to bring her son and daughter to join us for the evening feast.

It was a grand meal indeed. Naomi sang Christmas carols. Davey cooed along with her, as if struggling to sing a duet with his Mother. I made a corncob doll for him, which he fiercely held onto throughout the day.

After we ate, Garland read the Christmas story from the Bible. I glimpsed at Naomi when he read the passage about Mary laying her child in a manager. I wondered what Mary's neighbors and friends must have thought about her, for wasn't she, too, pregnant and unwed when she gave birth to Jesus?

Before the evening ended, Friends showed up, six of them who attended the same meeting house we did. I'm sure they were surprised to see me sitting there, holding an infant.

They looked from one to the other. Ellen, one of the women, sniffed loudly.

Garland, taking charge, said, "I'd like all of you to meet the newest member of our family. We've named him David.

One of the women, looking at the others, opened her mouth. I feared she would interrupt with questions before Garland could continue.

"David is an orphan child with no relative to take care of him right now. We've taken him on."

Then, without thought, words so familiar to me flowed

from my mouth: "Our people shall be his people."

Naomi glanced at me and smiled.

Arabelle brought in chestnuts she'd roasted on the fire. Garland opened a bottle of his prized muscadine wine. I hugged Davey tightly. How would I ever let him go?

Thirteen

"Great joy abounding" is how I remember the next two years.

I teased Garland, telling him he'd grown a green thumb. The crops were abundant; the livestock increased threefold. He built onto our log cabin adding a large separate room. Most startling of all, he apparently took pleasure in every minute of every day. Finally, he had wrestled free of the black moods and headaches that once plagued him. The obstacles we'd faced together apparently softened his temperament. Even being constantly surrounded by women no longer aggravated him. Best of all, he now had Davey in his corner.

Looking at the two of them together thrilled my heart. In all my days, I'd never known any man who needed a child more than Garland. Even though Davey, now three, was too young to be of help, he trotted behind my husband to the barn. After returning, he amused us by making animal noises. Short in stature, he had a round little belly which he amply filled.

If Garland ate cornpone, Davey ate it too. Once day Garland cut off a piece of red hot pepper to add to his beans. Despite our protests, Davey insisted on having some on his. All of us explained how hot it would be, but he grabbed a sliver anyway. After he gobbled it up, he howled, tears running down his chubby cheeks.

When I offered him a dipper of water, he drank all of it and begged for more. Despite his devotion to Garland, Davey never ate hot peppers again.

Over time, Naomi grew more accustomed to living among the Society of Friends. During her sixteenth year, she actually grew even more beautiful. She pulled back her long dark hair and twisted it into a neat bun. Her dark eyes, staring intently from her heart-shaped face, sought and still found natural wonders everywhere: A spider web, silvered by sunlight, the song of a lark; fireflies, plentiful as stars on warm evenings. Her laughter, though less shrill now, often rang out across the meadow. Just as she'd done when still a little girl, she often turned round and round on windy days and rolled on the ground when the weather turned warm.

Thankfully, being around us had rubbed off some of her rough edges. She learned to speak politely to others. Though she spent little time reading, Her word skills slowly improved. From Arabelle, Naomi learned how to find herbs and roots as well as how to treat people with them. Still her greatest joy came from tending the hens and cows.

She even developed an obsession for cleanliness. When not in the garden, she kept her fingernails clean and carried a handkerchief in her pocket to take care of a runny nose. Her zeal for housework and her creative bent with decorating and cooking enlivened our existence. Blessed with seemingly endless energy, she eagerly joined Garland in the field, whenever needed, helping him plant and harvest crops.

Though so much meanness had surrounded her early on, she appeared to have escaped the smudge. Though she had a right to be sad, I'd rarely encountered anyone happier. She seemed to resent nothing, even willingly let Garland and me spend all the time we wished with her son. She even agreed to the name Garland selected for her son. "David's a fine name," she said. "But, as for me, I'll never call him Davey."

Arabelle obviously admired Naomi. "That girl know the value of doing," she said, nodding her head. "She weave happiness for herself. She don't let bad thoughts mess up her mind like some folks be doing."

Looking down, I examined my hands. Sometimes my fingers trembled. Was it because of the bad thoughts I let creep in? Craving to partake of Arabelle's wisdom, I peered into her dark eyes. "So," I asked, "never allowing bad thoughts to enter one's mind is a good thing?"

She shook her head. "Not always." she said. "The mind be a door. If we always deny bad thoughts entry, they might crash through."

Shivering, I stood up to search for the blue shawl I rarely wore except on snowy evenings.

One late afternoon as I sat with my husband drinking tea, Garland commented on how valuable Naomi had become to us. "I don't know how we ever got along without her. In the garden she does the work of a man and she has an uncanny understanding of animals."

"Yes, I know."

With his knife, he shaved off more wood from the small piece of oak he had selected to form into a whistle for Davey. "How difficult life must be for an orphan. No dowry. No prospects. We should give Naomi something that would be her own."

"What a generous idea."

"Cal Whitstone offered to sell me his stallion, the one I've long admired. I'm thinking of buying it if he'll let it go for a good price. If I do, we could hook the new horse to the carriage when we go to meetings, and I could give the gray mare to Naomi."

"Oh, Garland. You know how fond of Sadie that girl is. She'd love it."

I walked over to my husband. "You know, these last two year has been so perfect, almost too perfect."

Putting his arms around me, he whispered, "Never question God's blessings, Mary Ruth, just accept them."

As winter rolled into spring and spring into summer, our days remained tranquil and productive. Arabelle still helped on the farm, and since Garland increased the acreage to be plowed, her son Wilmont and her daughter Jewel also helped out.

Naomi told us her birthday was in August. She didn't actually know which day, so we decided to celebrate the beginning of her seventeenth year on the fifth day of the month. Though Friends' celebrations are simple, there's always ample food. For dessert, I sliced some of the peaches I'd gathered from our trees and added cream. Little Davey sweetly sang a song he made up.

Could we ever allow him to call her mother, I wondered. Would we tell him someday? If Naomi suffered from his lack of attention, she never once let on. Indeed she treated Davey much as a big sister would treat a younger sibling. Sometimes she sang and played games with him, but most of the time she remained too preoccupied with house or yard work to pay him much mind.

Arabelle's gift to Naomi was a gourd she'd painted green, blue, and red. She said those three colors represented prosperity, tranquility and love. Naomi squealed with delight. Since the top of the gourd had been removed and the seeds scooped out, she declared it would be perfect for holding some of her treasures.

There's something else for you, Naomi," I told her. "But to receive it, you'll have to agree to be blindfolded."

No one loved a game more than her, but Davey protested, "I want blindfold too."

To shush him, I ripped up strips of a discarded apron to tie around both his and Naomi's eyes. Garland lifted Davey and Naomi held onto my arm as we stumbled down the familiar path.

"Where are you?" Garland asked, once we reached our destination.

Davey sniffed. When he said, "Moo cow," we laughed.

"What do you think, Naomi?"

She pinched her nose. "We're definitely near the barn."

"Tell me, what do you think your gift might be?" I asked

"Moo cow," Davey said again.

"Well, my lad," Garland said, "if you milk moo cow every day for the next ten years, consider her yours. How about it, Naomi? What do you think?"

She shook her head.

"We've teased her enough," I said. "Take the blindfold off, Dear."

By the time, she uncovered her eyes, Garland had the grey mare by the reins, coaxing her outside. When he announced, "Sadie's yours," I swear I thought Naomi would pop right open.

Then, doubting, she shook her head. "Not really?"

"Yes, really," Garland said. "From now on no one will ride her but you. She's yours to look after, care for, and go places.

With the gift, Naomi became one of us. Early on, she'd learned to scrub away the dirt and grime from her face and hands; now her kindnesses to others washed away her past. To my own eyes, she physically resembled us more than the people across the river. "What else might I do to help," were words she frequently spoke. Her eagerness to be useful won our hearts again and again.

I explained to her that she had a choice. If she so desired, she could attend the monthly Society of Friends meetings, but we had no right to require her to do so. For a while, she attended, proudly riding Sadie. Though a bit shy around strangers, she did her best to blend in with the other women. The men, during those years, met in a separate room. After several months, apparently gaining insight from the meditations, Naomi rose up once and spoke, saying "I, too, feel an inner light burning within me."

I noticed a few of the others looking at one another, as if she had no business to speak thus. Though I understood their reservations, for she represented to them what was outside, I resented their hesitancy in accepting her. Wasn't the belief that all people had rights at the very root of our faith? Didn't good Quakers even speak out for the rights of Indians and blacks?

Following the separate meetings, we women walked outside joining the men. One Sunday a stranger showed up. The man was tall with regular features. His brown scraggly hair flopped down covering his eyebrows. I did not approve his bold manner or the mustache hiding most of his upper lip. When he looked toward Naomi, he tipped his hat. His gaze resembled that of a man examining merchandise he planned to bid on at auction. Though a warm day, I shivered.

Naomi blushed and then quickly looked away. Though I hoped that would be the end of it, I feared otherwise. What would he think, I wondered, if he knew she had an illegitimate child?

After the service, she climbed on Sadie and rode off. I watched with unease as the stranger, after mounting his black steed, headed off in the same direction.

Garland, stood nearby, discussing gardening with neighbors. "It's been drier lately," I heard him say. We'll be in for it if we don't soon get a good soaking." The others voiced agreement, one or two of them even venturing when the next storm might come.

Walking up to my husband, I touched his sleeve. "Perhaps we should leave," I suggested. He must not have caught the urgency in my voice, for he still lingered. Turning from him, I headed for the carriage.

Should I tell Garland about the man following Naomi? I wondered. Before he caught up with me, I decided to say nothing. Perhaps Naomi and the unkempt young man heading in the same direction was a mere coincidence. Surely Naomi had sense enough to go straight home. Arabelle's daughter Jewel, only twelve years old, had agreed to keep an eye on Davey while we attended the service. Her mother would soon be expecting her home.

Naomi didn't speak of the mysterious stranger. But a few days later, Cora Weaver, came to my door. As usual her dress and apron were neat as a pin. She wore her modesty piece wrapped tightly about her neck. Though she claimed her hens had stopped laying, so she needed to borrow a few eggs, I suspected something else prompted the visit. Cora had been known to stir up trouble in the Society. When my neighbor Nellie died, she'd stretched the truth, claiming I'd agreed to stay with my friend during her long illness. As we walked toward the hens' nests, she asked if I remembered the tall stranger who attended the monthly meeting.

"Well, yes," I admitted.

"His name is Jonathan Lewis. He had no business being there. He's from the other side."

When I frowned, she clarified what she meant. "From across the river. His parents are part of the group who ventured here from down near the ocean. Worse than pirates, if you ask me. I heard his father killed his own brother. Can you imagine?"

Thoughts of Naomi's cruel uncle came to mind. I tried to subdue them. Weren't we wrong to judge people so harshly, based solely on how they dressed, what their beliefs might be, or from whence they came? Still the pit of my stomach ached with the knowing of the unknown. Whatever thoughts Jonathan Lewis had about our Naomi, they were not honorable.

Rain fell in torrents the afternoon I talked to Naomi. Though I feared my words would offend her, she sat quietly, stitching together quilt squares as I discussed the innate nature of men. They were different from us, I explained, but some men like Garland had learned from their parents and the community around them how to treat women properly.

Though I noticed she paused and looked up at me, I thought nothing of it, at least not then. I continued with information I felt she needed to know. "Some men are ignorant concerning the rules of society." Such men, I warned her, should be avoided.

Taking her hand, beautiful despite a callus she'd earned

from hard work, I talked on. "You uncle, I believe, was one of those men. He never learned to behave around others. He never cared for you properly."

Her answer startled me. "The Bible says anyone can be forgiven."

"I won't deny God's grace, Naomi, but you're a woman now, wise enough to avoid men who wish you harm."

"How will I recognize such men?" she asked.

"Your heart will tell you, but if you have any doubts, ask me."

"Is it Jonathan Lewis who disturbs you?"

I though of tip-toeing around the question, but didn't. Instead I offered her bold truth. "Yes. Have you talked to him?"

"Only once. The day he attended meeting. When he followed me, we stopped out by Adam's Spring. I explained to him I was an orphan. Since then I haven't seen hide or hair of him."

Though I despised being suspicious, I kept a close eye on Naomi. For days after our talk, I inquired about Jonathan Lewis whenever in company with other Quakers. I found out that he worked as a store clerk in nearby Asheboro, and that he still lived with his widowed mother. I also learned that his mother had encouraged him to court and marry Alice Henrickson, the younger sister of the store owner. That bit of news comforted me. Alice Henrickson's dowry would be doubtless be substantial. Why wouldn't any ambitious young man be tempted?

Yet how foolish of me to be comforted by such news. History reveals again and again how both young men and young women make illogical choices when they allow their emotions to take over. Think of Romeo and Juliet? Antony and Cleopatra? Kingdoms fall over decisions made for love or lust, so how could I have possibly believed it would be different with Jonathan Lewis, a rakish mustache hiding his upper lip, his tongue licking the lower as if already tasting victory.

    Was I to blame for all that later happened to Naomi? When, years later, I asked that question, my husband consoled me, "It wasn't you, Mary Ruth, or God."

Fourteen

By his fifth birthday, Davey behaved like a little man. Now that he spent more time with Garland than with either me or Naomi, he became my husband's ally against the women inhabiting the house. With great patience, Garland helped the boy learn to milk a cow and depress holes for planting during spring. When summer ripened the tomatoes, corn, and beans, he let Davey pick all he could reach.

Endowed with a stubborn streak, the dark-haired imp yowled until red-faced when my husband declared Davey wasn't old enough to gather fragile eggs. One evening, he marched inside our house anyway, carrying three of them. Davey spoke boldly. "I'm a big boy. I can do anything you can do, Papa."

Naomi and I covered our mouths to hide grins. Garland somehow managed to keep his face stern. "Young man, you might be able to gather eggs, but until you have my permission,

I forbid you to do so."

Knowing how much he loved Garland, I'm sure the words crushed Davey. When he came running to me, tears in his dark eyes, I opened my arms.

Naomi changed as well during those years. For her eighteenth birthday, Garland made her a small wooden chest, providing a place where she could keep the few items of clothing she wore. But Naomi had another use in mind. She began collecting items, as other young women her age were prone to do, that would be needed if she ever had a home of her own. Afraid of offending her, I didn't caution her concerning the folly of such thinking, still who would dare marry Naomi? Even if a man loved her enough to forgo a monetary reward for doing so, how would he react when he found out she had a bastard son?

Naomi made many of the items she carefully folded, placing in her chest, including a brightly colored quilt similar to the one she made for me. She also included two plates, the rims imprinted with red roses; a spoon; a chipped china cup and a ring, which appeared to be silver. When I asked where she'd gotten it, she looked away from me, claiming to have found it in the woods. Another find was arrowheads used by the Indians who'd once lived in the area. She hoped to trade those for enough material to make a nightgown.

I intended to have a long conversation with Naomi, assuring her she'd always have a place with us, but I never got around to it, for I discovered I was with child again.

Though this time, I didn't dare hope to birth a healthy infant, Garland insisted I have a proper doctor. Within the last year, Dr. Carl Odom, already established in Asheboro, took to riding over to our community one day a week. After visiting those who were ill, he would have the big meal of the day with one of the families in the area before returning home.

During one of the doctor's visits to our community, Garland invited him to our house without letting me know.

How young he looks, I thought when Dr. Odom entered our door. He hadn't yet reached an age when he could grow a full beard. His shifty eyes, a much paler shade of blue than Garland's, glanced here and there but never directly at me.

After enjoying the ham and rice we served him, the doctor dictated harsh rules which made little sense. I was to stay in bed until the birth. Garland would be allowed in the bedroom only briefly twice a day. Because of the unfortunate childbirths I'd experienced before, any activity could lessen the chances of carrying the child to term, he contended.

What should have been a happy time for me and my husband became insufferable. I was sick, worried, and constantly tormented by visions of my dead children. Though ashamed, I wished I were not burdened with carrying another babe. Wasn't Davey as close to my heart as any child of my own could possibly be?

Naomi worked relentlessly in the field; Arabelle summoned all her strength to help me. Still I saw sorrow everywhere. The clouds seemed to form shapes of dead children and tombstones. Most of the food I tried had a rancid taste, and over time, a smell of discontent filled every corner of the room. The one bright spot of each day was when Davey came in, climbing in bed beside me and requesting a story. "Where you been, Mama?" he'd ask. His question broke my heart.

Just when had he started calling me Mama? I wondered. Should I allow it?

When he crawled beneath the purple and blue quilt his mother made, I'd close my eyes thinking up a story to entertain him. Best of all, he enjoyed the ones I told about pirates. "Aye, aye, Captain," he'd say, interrupting me.

Too soon he'd be asleep next to me, his thumb stuck in his mouth. How I wanted him to stay there, but Arabelle would dutifully pick him up, carrying him away. "That doctor say it for your own good," she'd remind me.

By my fourth month of pregnancy, I finally perked up. My stomach no longer felt unsettled and the pain in my lower back lessened somewhat. "How I wish I could get up and go outside," I confessed to Arabelle. "If only I could walk to the river."

She touched my face, my arms, and my legs. She placed both her hands on my bulging stomach and closed her eyes. She became so quiet she seemed not to be there. Eventually she looked at me once more. "Everything seem to be as it should be," she said, a broad grin lighting up her face. "Getting up might be good for you. But mind you, just for a short while."

For the first time in weeks, my heart lifted. Placing her arm behind my back, she helped me get out of bed. Feeling a bit woozy, I took a deep breath before attempting to stand on my own feet. Gradually, excitement took over. If I'd been in prison for a decade and was suddenly released, I don't believe I would have felt any more elated.

Once outside, I sat once again in the chair Garland made for me. Looking up through the leaves overhead, I observed a flock of white doves flying past. The vision lifted my spirit. I felt the light within, I should be doing something useful. "Arabelle, please bring me paper and my quill?"

When she returned, I wasn't sure what I wished to write. "Everything I have actually belongs to Garland," I said to her.

"That the truth. Women got no rights."

"My husband has a kind heart. I don't believe he'd mind

if I make a few requests if I don't live to see my child."

"Don't be talking such. You be fine."

I stared her down. She placed her hands on her hips and shook her head before leaving to retrieve the supplies I needed.

Ink flowed onto paper as I specified my requests. Give Davey the storybook I had as a child and Naomi my Bible and the locket my mother gave me. "What do I have that you might want, Arabelle?"

"For you to behave yourself without this constant jabbering of sickness."

"That's what you told me before Belle's birth."

"I told you that baby be born a fine girl with curly yellow hair and it be just as I predicted. Sometime the message given be limited. Sometime I don't see far enough ahead. Even if I had seen, would it have helped to know?"

When unbidden tears dampened my eyes, I took a handkerchief from my pocket.

Arabelle talked on. "You gots to believe everything be fine. That's all any of us got—believing."

Making up my mind to heed her advice, I picked up my pen and began writing down all I loved about the world God had given me. I treasure the chestnut tree which bears fruit and attracts animals. After reading over what I'd written, I drew a line through the words. Though I did indeed love the chestnut tree, there was so much I loved more. Beginning again, I wrote, *I love little Davey and I'm grateful that my husband loves him as well. Please bless Naomi for sharing him with us.*

Before I completed my list, a shadow surrounded me. I glanced up, expecting to see the sun disappearing behind clouds. Then I heard a sound, someone breathing. Back from the field early?" I asked my husband. Looking down, I hoped I'd misinterpreted the flash of anger I glimpsed in his eyes.

He never answered my question. Instead he demanded I go back to bed. "Aren't you concerned for your unborn child?" he asked. "Or me? You know the doctor said you needed to remain in bed. I've done my part, though it's been difficult. I haven't once demanded you do your wifely duty during your waiting time. What can you be thinking, Mary Ruth, being outside like this?"

Oh, how his words stung. My face heated up; I heard the thumping of my heart. "I feel ever so much better out here, getting fresh air, not having to stare continually at four walls."

"Ah, so that's it? You take the word of a root woman over the advice of a trained doctor and your own husband. Well, I won't have you destroying my child. Get back inside." He lifted me from the chair by pushing up on my elbows. Though angry tears spread down my face, I didn't resist.

Once I stumbled back inside, he confronted Arabelle. "It was your duty to make sure my wife stayed in bed."

"She had nothing to do with it," I said.

"Arabelle, we won't be needing you anymore."

My mouth dropped open. This was not the Garland I'd married. Oh, he'd always been a bit stern, always keeping his spine straight, but the husband I thought I'd married had been reasonable. He'd actually stood at meetings, speaking from his heart, as he admonished the cruel treatment of blacks and Indians. Now, for no reason, except that to his mind she was different, strange, harboring beliefs he couldn't comprehend, he demanded that Arabelle leave.

I bit my lip, determined to forego more tears.

After Garland left, Arabelle attempted to comfort me as she gathered her belongings. "It be all right, Mary Ruth. I got plenty that needs doing at home and Mrs. Hilliard say any time I got time, she could use me. Before I leave I be speaking to Naomi, telling her how to take care of you."

"Now you be calming yourself down. Mr. Eversole be doing this for your own good. He so concern about that baby, he ain't got his head on straight. I'll tell Naomi to keep the window open, making certain you get air, except at night time. Sometimes bad things come flying in after dark."

Arabelle limped toward me. I recalled the horrible story she'd once told me about the slave owner hitting her with a stick, breaking her leg. She took my hand, felt the pulse in my wrist. Rising up, I placed my arms around her. "This will change," I said. "He'll be asking you to come back."

"Don't worry your mind bout nothing but yourself and your baby." Those were the final words of the strong woman I'd come to depend on, believe in, and yes, love.

Naomi brought me chicken soup that evening and hot tea. "Where is Garland?" I asked.

She rubbed my shoulders, but offered no explanation. "Is there anything else I can do for you?" she asked. "Anything at all?" Looking in her eyes, I saw sorrow almost as deep as the sadness I'd seen before when she had been beaten and left in the road. "What is it, Naomi?"

She talked on, avoiding my question. "There are peaches, if you'd like one. I few ripened today."

"No, thank you, Dear," I managed before I sought the comfort of my pillow. Those whom I thought loved me were making no sense. Why were Naomi and Garland acting so strangely? Surely it had to be something more serious than my getting out of bed.

The next day Dr. Odom came to check on me again. Without giving the poor man a chance, I lit into him, "This was Garland's idea, wasn't it? He asked you to come by."

He smiled, then turned to look out the open window. "You should keep the window closed, especially on rainy days."

Resentment welled up in me. Women had babies, not men, so why was it that men considered themselves authorities on childbirth. Both Garland and the doctor spoke quietly, clearly, attempting to calm me, but their words didn't matter. "If I did stay in bed during the entire pregnancy, how would I manage to get up once the child was born?" I asked. Though I tried visualizing the child alive and well, I couldn't and, truth to tell, didn't even want to. If I imagined the worst now, when this baby joined its other siblings in death, wouldn't it hurt less? If I had no expectations, perhaps I would be spared some of the pain.

Finally, the doctor agreed that I could walk about for brief periods in the room, but I should never, under any circumstances, go downstairs or outside on my own. Turning to Garland, he said, "Carry her out once a week provided the weather isn't too humid. It will be good for both of you to sit together for a while, and will be worth the risk if it prevents your wife from becoming unduly upset."

The doctor took my hand. "Believe me, I do understand. Carrying a child is always emotional for women. Given your medical history, it's particularly important for you to stay calm." Before leaving, he instructed I should drink or eat only the foods on the list he'd given to Naomi.

Instead of working in the fields as she'd done previously, Naomi, at Garland's request, spent most of her time with either me or Davey. Though I missed Arabelle and worried about her, my relationship with Naomi gradually resumed its former rhythm. At first, she spoke rarely, but soon, accepting what we could not change, we relaxed enjoying one another's company. We sewed, took turns reading to one another, and she daily massaged my back, always sore from spending so much time in bed.

I was actually pleased that she now played frequently with her son, for as the doctor reminded me, this pregnancy threatened my own life as well the infant's. Though saddened that I might not be around to see Davey grow and thrive, I was grateful that if I did not, his birth mother would be there for him.

Fifteen

During the next few months, as my own body grew more cumbersome, I noticed that Naomi had also put on weight and looked unwell. "Are you sick?" I asked her one morning.

She looked away from me. "Tired is all."

I blamed Garland. He'd banished Arabelle for no good reason and left Naomi in charge of all the household chores plus looking after me. "Do you miss being outside?"

"I'm happy being with you, Ruthie," she said, but her words didn't fool me. I sensed her pain and disappointment. She no longer searched for treasures to carefully tuck in her dowry chest. Instead she searched for items to amuse either me or Davey.

One dreary morning, I heard an unexpected knock on the door. Who might it be, I wondered. Probably not one of the women in the community. They rarely came by and certainly not in the morning. Behaving as if they believed unsuccessful childbirth was contagious, a few even avoided me entirely.

I heard Naomi walk toward the door and unlatch it. Then a squeal and positive words of greeting flew up the stairs. It had to be Arabelle. I felt sure of it even before she labored up the stairs.

Opening my arms to her, I smiled. "I wasn't expecting you," I said, "But, oh, my Dear, I'm so grateful you're here."

As she drew closer, her presence scented the room with ginger and pine. "I won't stay long, but the stars and moon be demanding I make a call. Both you and Naomi need me."

"I, too, have been concerned for Naomi. She doesn't look well."

"I look over you first," my tall friend said, "while Naomi be cooking up food I brought."

After touching my stomach tenderly, she smiled. "The baby be fine," she said.

"Are you sure?" I asked.

"You need to believe for the good of your daughter. Your feelings bleed through to her."

"Daughter?" I smiled. You know how I would love having a girl child to teach, to guide." I took Arabelle's wrinkled hand into my own. "But tell me, how can I be hopeful considering my past history."

"We be whatever we choose. We each have the power within to make it so." Arabelle spoke in a whisper; her dark eyes drilling the truth into me. "Drink the root tea Naomi be making for you. That will lift the darkness traveling over your soul."

As she rubbed my hands and feet with her large hands, she chanted words I didn't comprehend.

Who was I to believe? Where did my loyalty belong? Should I listen to this strange woman, her background so different from my own, or to my own dear husband, whom

I'd known for most of my life?

"Meditate," Arabelle advised. "Consult the light that be within for an answer."

"I smiled, "Why Arabelle, have you become a Quaker?"

"I be what I need to be to convince folks what the moon and stars be telling."

"What's wrong with Naomi?" I asked for the second time. "Do the stars and the moon tell you that?"

"I need no stars or moon. That be simple. She be like you."

"In what way?"

"With child."

The possibility of such a thing never entered my head. I'm not sure why. The symptoms had been clear for several months. The nausea, the tiredness.

A great ball of anger welled up in me. I burrowed my head in my pillow. Though I listened to Arabelle's slow even breathing, I found no solace. When finally I lifted my head and looked up, my cinnamon-skinned friend was there for me, tears in her eyes, opening her arms.

Who was the father? That's the question I wanted answered. The uncle was dead, so it couldn't have been him. I remembered Jonathan Lewis, the roustabout from the Eastern part of the state who had once shown up in the midst of a Quaker meeting, but that had been over a year ago. Still, the way he'd stared at Naomi with such lust made him the most likely possibility. Why hadn't Naomi listened when I warned her about him? Despite my deep love and concern for her, I wanted to grab her and shake some sense into her head. Then fear took over. When Garland found out, would he make her leave?

Arabelle poured a drop or two of almond-scented oil onto her fingertips and touched my forehead, each cheek, my chin.

"Don't fret so," she said.

Within a few minutes Naomi came up the stairs, carrying tea. She kept her head down as she handed it to me. I recall taking only one sip. Sleep came quickly, freeing me, at least temporarily, from frantic thoughts.

I rested for the entire day, and awoke feeling renewed. How easy following Arabelle's mandate had been. How I wished I could be like her, offering gifts of acceptance and forgiveness to others, especially Garland and Naomi. What I could give them, had to give them, was truth. First, I would speak to Naomi, informing her that I knew she was with child, begging her to reveal the name of the father. Then I would speak to Garland, insisting he let Naomi stay despite any indiscretion. I recalled again, the vow I first made to my husband, "My people shall be thy people" and how later, when Naomi came to live with us, I'd said the same words to her. Though I didn't always approve of how either of them behaved, I knew I would never break my vow to either of them.

On the following Monday, as Naomi tended me, she avoided conversation. Garland, who stayed busy tending the crops and animals, was never in the house long enough to talk. On Tuesday, finally, a long awaited rain came, keeping him inside the house. He would spend the time with me, he said, and give Naomi some rest.

As he sat beside me in bed that morning, reading scripture, I noticed new wrinkles in his deeply tanned face. The wrinkles didn't alarm me as much as the way the corners of his mouth sagged.

"What's wrong?" I asked.

When I touched him to determine if he might have a fever, I noticed that his forehead felt damp. He pushed my hand away. "I might ask the same of you, Mary Ruth."

I did not hesitate. The words, moldy from having been

locked in my mind so long, tumbled out. Though I'd intended to begin with revealing Naomi's predicament, I spoke first of Arabelle. "The baby will be coming sometime during the next two months. I want Arabelle to be here when it happens. The death of our last child had nothing to do with her or what she might have done. I trust her."

His eyes opened wide, as if surprised. "For all we know, she might be practicing witchcraft."

"You know better, Garland."

His mouth became a stern line. "She didn't obey the doctor's orders. You have a delicate disposition, Mary Ruth. You can't be treated as just any woman."

"If I'm forced to remain continually in bed, I will surely die."

"The doctor I'm paying to look after you has studied medicine. He knows what's best."

"He's a man, Garland. How can I be expected to wholly trust a man's insights concerning the treatment of women?"

When he sighed, I knew I had a chance. "Allow Arabelle to come back. I fear for my child if she's not here."

He shook his head.

"Please, listen to me and listen to your own heart. Shouldn't I be the one deciding what help I need? I know and the child inside me knows, I must have Arabelle."

His face became stony, hard. When he didn't answer, I brought up the other matter troubling my heart.

"Have you noticed any change in Naomi?" I asked.

He squirmed in the chair. "Why do you ask?"

"She's with child, Garland."

Color rose in his cheeks. "Are you certain?"

"She hasn't actually told me, but it's apparent. That's another reason I need Arabelle. Naomi needs to be looking after herself, not just me."

I'd rarely seen my husband look so perplexed. I was the misfit, the one who usually panicked in awkward situations. As he ran his fingers through his hair, my heart went out to him.

"I don't know who the father is," I said. "I plan to have a talk with Naomi. I suspect it might be Jonathan Lewis, one of those young men who live across the river. Remember, he came to meeting once. I warned Naomi about him."

Garland banged his fist on the arm of the chair. "Those living on the other side of Deep River have joined league with the devil."

I had never before heard my husband express such thoughts against anyone or anything. By nature, he was the peacemaker, making allowances, forgiving, as a good Quaker should.

He cleared his throat. "So," he said, "if you insist on having Arabelle, what shall we do with Naomi?"

"We made a vow to keep her, to care for her. Then, sensing I had the advantage, I added, "If she leaves, she'll take Davey with her."

As if in agony, he placed his head in his hands, then, looking up, finally relented. "How can I deny you anything, Mary Ruth?"

Smiling, I took his rough hand and kissed it.

Though pleased to get my way, I was confused. Long ago, I'd been told never to waste time worrying about what someone else might be thinking, for there was no way to know. For the first time, I experienced a great chasm separating Garland and me. Perhaps I'd never known my husband at all.

"I'm tired. I need to rest now." Actually, I felt strong enough, but felt no desire to be near him. Finding the soft hollow in my pillow, the place where I always sought sleep, I planned what I would say to Naomi.

Sixteen

Naomi, her eyes twinkling with excitement, brought me a peach. Blushed by sun, the fuzzy skin though deep pink still retained a bit of yellow. I held the delicate fruit to my nose. "Few things smell better," I said. "No other fruit tastes quite so delicious."

"Tis true," she agreed. Taking the peach from me, she peeled it with a knife and fed it to me as if I were a child.

"Make sure Davey gets a taste."

Before putting the last delectable slice in her own mouth, she assured me that by day's end, there'd be enough peaches for all of us to enjoy one.

When I wrote down my daily account of all I loved, fresh peaches would top the list. For now, I needed to have a serious talk with Naomi. She was too smart to blurt out the truth if I confronted her directly. I had to find another way.

"Naomi," I said, "you've put on a bit of weight lately. Is it because my husband has forced you to stay with me? I know you must miss being outside."

She looked down at the dusty black boots covering her feet. I remembered again how spunky she'd once been. "You know, don't you?" she asked.

"Yes, I believe I do." Rising from the bed, I embraced my friend.

"Please, don't." Tears trickled down her cheeks. "You're supposed to rest."

"Yes, and you were supposed to stay away from Jonathan Lewis. I warned you about him. When Garland and I took you in, we explained that you must separate yourself from those on the other side of the river."

"It wasn't him." She spoke so softly, I barely heard the words.

Should I believe her? "Who else could it have been?"

She did not speak. I was once again reminded of her behavior before Davey's birth, continually refusing to give out any information concerning the father. I knew by the set of her jaw I wouldn't receive an answer this time either. I turned from her, attempting to hide my anger. Naomi took my cool hand into her own. "What if Garland forces you to leave?" I asked her.

Unvoiced emotions, both mine and Naomi's, leapt about the room. Closing my eyes, I imagined our intense feelings staining the walls yellow, red, black. I felt a sharp pain in my stomach. Perhaps it was my own unborn daughter punishing me for opening up a can of worms.

Resigned, knowing I'd have to attempt getting an answer some other way, I spoke of another matter. "Garland says that Arabelle can come back and stay with me. Would you find her for me and let her know?"

Two days later, I was ecstatic when I heard my wise friend

enter the house. The banging downstairs was surely her opening windows, letting in air. Soon her shoes clomped on the stairs. I grinned when she walked through the door, but she didn't grin back. With her hands on her hips, she let me know she'd considered not coming. "I won't be forgiving, Mr. Eversole," she declared boldly. "No, this time he went too far. I'm not here because he allow me to be. No, my reason is cause you need me."

Though I knew I should defend my husband's decision to let her go, I didn't. Instead, I bowed my head, thanking God for bringing her back. When I took her rough hand into my own, I felt the light of truth inside my breast reassuring me, that with her help, the child I was expecting would be okay.

"Quakers talk a good talk," Arabelle said, "but when it get close to home, they seem to forget what they believe. That what I think got into Mr. Eversole. "Yeah, the Master done lost a piece of his soul."

I felt blood rushing to my face. "Please, don't do this, Arabelle. My husband respects you. He asked you to leave because he didn't understand your beliefs."

"He believe in what he knows, calling it God. Maybe I do the same. My God just be different from his." Turning from me, she walked to the window and yanked open the curtains.

"Won't that doctor let you look at trees?" she asked. Anger distorted her face.

"Of course I can look at trees," I said which was only half true. The doctor's orders were that the thick curtains be closed during the heat of the day. "You know how I love them, particularly the chestnut tree. It still attracts so many animals."

"It's easier to love trees than people."

"Yes," I agreed. "A tree only disappoints if there's a storm or disease. Those reasons can't be controlled so they're easily forgiven."

We spoke of how fortunate we'd been to have so much rain. "I understand the river's full," I said. "It must be beautiful."

"It be scary," she answered. "If more rain come, it rise above the banks."

When I asked her to describe my baby to me, she gently placed her hands on my stomach and closed her eyes. "A girl. I've already told you that. Her hair will be blond and curly. Her eyes blue."

"Like Belle. Then she'll look like Garland?"

"Yes, but her nature will resemble your own." When she saw me frown, she added, "Mary Ruth, that be a good thing. You blessed with compassion on the heart. That be your gift. Don't let no one tear it from you."

Her fierceness startled me. But then her eyes quickly softened again and a smile curled up the corners of her mouth. Taking my hand, she asked me to close my eyes and repeat after her. "The calmness be washing over me, bringing peace to the girl child within. She be a beautiful child, a child of light." When my baby kicked, I laughed. Arabelle joined me, giggling as if she knew exactly what had happened.

Soon I fell asleep, dreaming of my daughter. I saw her at age six trying to learn her numbers. Sitting in my lap, she watched as I wrote each one, then named it quickly. When I wrote thirteen, she asked. "What is that number? What does it mean?"

Despite the puzzling vision, I awoke feeling refreshed. I'd speak to Arabelle. I'd beg her to let me go outside. I wanted to smell the roses in my garden. I wanted to plant new blossoms. But, as I found out later, she had already left. When Naomi bought tea to me, she explained that Garland her instructed her to leave, but had given permission for her to return the following day.

Seventeen

Afternoon rest provided no cure. My bones ached and my left leg cramped from remaining so much in bed. Even worse, anxiety took hold. Awful images of death and hopelessness filled my dreams; images I dared not speak of for fear they might materialize. Exhausted both physically and mentally, I wondered once again how this torture of being confined to bed could possibly benefit my unborn child.

I called out to Naomi. When she reached the top step, I argued for my release from the prison my room had become.

Frowning, she turned aside. "We must both do as we're told."

I stared her down, forcing her to look at me. She shook her head. "If I had the freedom to do so, I would do as you ask, Ruthie, but I don't. I will open the window so you can get a bit of air. We'll have to hope your husband and the doctor don't find out."

As she pushed at the window, I asked about Garland.

"He's gone to a Society meeting. He said he wouldn't be home until late."

Deciding to make the best of this rare opportunity, I decided to push truth to light, clearing up concerns that weighed heavy on my heart. Once, Naomi and I had been so close. Though totally different in so many ways, I always valued her presence, and I think she valued mine as well. At least, she seemed to.

After Davey's birth, our friendship became strained. Discovering she was again pregnant widened the gap even more. I missed her; I wanted to trust her again. "Naomi," I said, "make yourself a cup of tea and join me. Remember how we used to have such long talks. When you were learning to read, you were curious about everything."

"Squirrels are curious. It often gets them in trouble." When she smiled, I closed my eyes, remembering how she used to twirl around and around on windy days. She still radiated such youth and warmth. I marveled how well she looked despite all she'd been through.

As I heard the sound of her sturdy shoes descending the stairs, I pondered what I'd say when she returned. Should I stick to small talk or should I get to the big question? By the time she placed the cup on the table beside the bed, I'd planned exactly what to say, but before I opened my mouth, she spoke, "What would you like to eat? I want to fix something special just for you?"

"Do we still have any of the sour pickles I put up in jars?"

"I think so."

"They're what I crave most, so please bring me a pickle, maybe two. That will suffice for me, along with a bit of bread, but make sure Garland gets meat."

Neither of us spoke again for at least a minute. I looked around the room. My eyes first rested on the washbowl and pitcher decorated with yellow flowers. I had traveled with it all the way from Pennsylvania, bringing it to this place in the wilderness, here where Garland and I made our life. I picked up a necklace made of hickory nuts and acorns from the table. Arabelle had given it to me. "This will give you all the courage you need," she told me. Hoping to bolster my self-assurance, I pulled the necklace over my head as the small clock on the bureau ticked, ticked, ticked. My father had given the curious instrument to Garland to mark the day of our marriage.

Naomi's head was lowered. With a large needle, she added stitches to a sampler. "Say the words you need to say," she said. "If you're angry with me and want me to leave, have out with it."

"I'm not mad, Naomi, and you're needed here, so I certainly don't want you to leave. What saddens me is that your secrets have separated us. Why won't you reveal the name of the father of this baby you're expecting? Was he Davey's father as well?"

She placed her hands, calloused by work, over her face. The clock ticked, ticked, ticked. Finally, she removed her hands, yet still didn't look at me. "I will give you the name of Davey's father, but only on one condition. Silence the questions concerning the child I now carry in my womb. Never will I let that name be known. It would serve no good purpose."

In my heart, I still believed, though she'd denied the truth of it, that Jonathan had fathered this second child. Of course, she'd be embarrassed to admit the truth, for I'd warned her repeatedly to stay away from him. "All right, Naomi, I won't ask for more information than you're willing to give. Though I wish you trusted me enough to tell everything, I can see that's not true. I've always feared your own uncle was Davey's father. Is that true?

Her cheeks turned red. Biting her lip, she nodded.

"Though I thought myself prepared for the answer, I gasped.

Tears flowed down Naomi's cheeks. I wanted to go to her, take her in my arms and comfort her. "Oh, Naomi, I'm so sorry."

"I couldn't help it. There wasn't anything I could do to stop him." Brushing tears aside with the back of her hand, she took a deep breath. "That's not all of it. I believe he raped my mother as well."

Closing my eyes, I tried to block out the brutality. I worried about the consequences of incest. I'd heard of cousins who married. Sometimes their children were born cross-eyed or with an extra kidney or not quite right in the head. Thank God, Davey appeared to be healthy and bright. Silently I prayed he wouldn't be affected by the sins of his father. I prayed for Naomi, too. The messiness of it sickened me.

Then another thought, even more horrible. "Naomi, you didn't kill him, did you?"

"Kill who?"

"Your uncle."

When she sobbed, I worried that she'd confess she'd done just that. I knew that if I'd been raped by such a man I would have killed him. Yes, killed him and damned him to hell.

"Ruthie, I've never been able to kill anything. You, more than anyone, should know that."

Thinking on it, I recalled that once Garland asked her to wring the neck of a chicken and chop its head off with an axe. After he left, Naomi threw up. My heart went out to her that day as on so many other days. I'd finally killed the chicken myself.

There was other evidence. She'd catch a frog, but then let it go. She never went along with us when we took Davey fishing, though she would always clean the brim and catfish when we brought them home. I'd watched butterflies land on her hand. Fascinated, she'd study the winged creature, but, unlike others I'd observed, never attempted to lift one by a wing.

Placing my feet on the floor, I rose up out of the bed. My legs felt rubbery, unstable. "I'd forgotten, my dear, how kind you've always been to God's creatures. Of course, you'd be incapable of killing your uncle." When she looked up at me, I smiled. "Why you can't even stomp a bug." I remembered once, when a baby squirrel fell from a tree, she'd gently picked it up and placed it in her pocket, hoping against hope it would survive.

Hearing someone coming up the steps, I hobbled back to bed. Naomi rushed to the window, intending to close it, but before she could, Garland walked in, looking first at her, then at me.

Before Naomi could say a word, I said, "While Naomi went to get me tea, I opened the window."

Running his long fingers through his blond hair, he glanced at the empty tea cups. Exasperation marked his tone. "Should I give up tending the farm and stay with you every minute of every day to make certain you follow the doctor's orders?"

Knowing that I would not be able to make him understand, I turned away. "Thank you for all your help today, Naomi. Garland, I think I'll get some sleep now."

After they left, I didn't sleep. Instead, I imagined myself small, curled up in a fetal position, all thoughts turned inward. The horror I'd experienced upon finding the uncle's body filled my head again. Reliving the experience, I tried to come up with an answer. It must have been some of his own people, I had to believe. No one here among in the community of Friends would kill another person. Such an act would defy all we believed. Perhaps Jonathan Lewis was the murderer. Perhaps he'd wanted Naomi even then.

In truth, I eventually discovered that Jonathan had committed no major crime during that particular time. It was his family's reputation, clinging to him like a dark shadow that made me suspicious. I'd heard the tale, vividly told, of how his own father killed Jonathan's uncle. He'd simply followed him home, pushed his rifle through the window and shot again and again. One woman told me the family closed off the bedroom after the crime. "Too horrible to contemplate," she said.

I objected when people judged Naomi harshly, perhaps I, too, was unjust in judging Jonathan. Still, though no proof existed, how could I squelch my intuition.

Eighteen

September, usually a gentle month in Piedmont, North Carolina, blew in fast and furious. The trees, like brightly garbed women, wiggled in the wind until their gold and red leaves gained freedom, blowing away. By the middle of October, all the tomatoes along with beans and corn disappeared from the garden. Only cabbages, pumpkins and apples remained.

On the twentieth day of the month, a fierce storm attacked our community. Slender pine trees broke one after the other. The sounds were menacing as blasts of a rifle. I looked out my bedroom window, trying to remain calm for the sake of my unborn child. A black roiling cloud filled the sky. It's nature's way, I thought. Soon the storm will be over, and we'll thank God for the much needed rain. Even before I got to Amen, a huge limb, which broke off from the trunk of my favorite chestnut trees crashed through the roof. I screamed.

Wet branches and twigs drenched the quilt and pillows on my bed. Rain continued to pour through the hole in the roof.

Trembling, I rubbed my arms. If I'd been in the bed, where my husband expected me to be, I would have been crushed.

Where was Garland? Where was Naomi? Pulling a black shawl around me, I moved around pieces of wood covering my bed. Reaching the stairs, I took one careful step, then another. Walking no longer seemed natural to me. I felt woozy and light-headed. When I tried reaching the next step, I missed, tumbling down the remaining five. Oddly, my mind relaxed despite the fall. I placed my hands against my stomach, willing my unborn child to be all right.

Later, I was told by Garland that I'd been unconscious by the time he and Naomi found me. They'd both been outside seeing to the livestock and picking up apples and pumpkins from the ground, hoping to save whatever they could.

By the time, I came to, I'd lost my baby.

"Boy or girl?" My words were like rough stones.

Naomi looked away. I'd miscarried, Garland explained gently.

"Boy or girl?"

Naomi, her eyes wide with terror, put her hand to her throat, then walked toward me tentatively, as if dreading to get there.

She rubbed my hand. "Ruthie," she said. "I'm so sorry I wasn't here."

"I am too. If you'd been here, I would have been in bed when the tree crashed through the roof. I would have died with my baby."

As she sobbed, hiding her face in her hands, I asked again, "Boy or girl? You have to know. How can I properly name my child if no one tells me?"

Naomi putting her arms around me, attempted to calm me down. "Ruthie, the baby was a girl. I'm sure of it."

Though I knew she lied, I accepted her answer for both

our sakes. "Then she'll be named Sarah," I said. "Sarah, after my saintly mother."

Such a cruel month. In addition to the roof of our home caving in, we lost the remaining crops, a half dozen chickens and three full-grown hogs. Still, if my child had only survived, all the other losses wouldn't have mattered. But the loss of my baby, without even seeing her sweet face, was almost more than I could bear.

I slept on the floor located on the lower level of our cabin. The next morning I refused to eat but accepted the cup of tea brought by Naomi. "They'll never do such a thing to me again," I said to her.

"Do what?" she asked.

"If ever again I'm fortunate enough to be with child, I'll do what I think best. We always make that mistake, don't we? Listening to men instead of listening to our own hearts. Go find Arabelle. Make sure she and her children are all right. Tell her to come if she can."

The house was cold and damp. Though distraught, Naomi managed to get the fire going. I had no idea where Garland might be. For a few awful hours, I had no desire to ever see him again.

When Arabelle arrived two days later carrying her basket of magic, we embraced, both of us sobbing. And that was the last of it, the last day I cried over the loss of a child. There was too much work to be done to allow room for grief. During the rest of October, we diligently toiled from sun up until sundown. I relished the work. Keep moving no matter what, I decided. That was the only way to live successfully on this earth. I vowed I'd never stop working from sun up to sun down again. If I kept busy, there would never again be a moment for sorrow to nest in my soul.

Davey became our bright light during those months. Old enough to understand holidays, he enjoyed the stories we told him about the pilgrims who had settled our country. He enjoyed even more the descriptions of the Indians who wore bright beads around their necks. With some help from Naomi, we made small turkeys out of pinecones and brought in colorful gourds for display. Garland made birdhouses and dippers from the larger ones. Those evenings around the fire, as I watched Garland tease Davey, some of the resentment I felt began to melt away. Davey calling me "Mama," kissed my cheek each morning. We played with a top Garland made and beat on pots pretending we were drummers. Being with that bright-eyed boy with such a beguiling grin restored me. Eventually I breathed free and easy once more.

Sometimes I glimpsed Naomi as she watched me playing pat-a-cake or some other child's game with her son. Did I glimpse envy in her eyes? Yes, I had lost four children, but Naomi had also lost a child. Her Davey had become ours. Would I ever be able to bear giving him back to her? And, if so, would she want him?

The men of the community had already helped Garland remove the Goliath tree limb from the top of our house. During most of November they hammered and sawed, replacing the damaged boards before adding a roof of sturdy tin. Naomi looked after cooking our meals as well as the house cleaning and washing. "Sit down and rest," I frequently reminded her, but unlike the treatment I received, I never mandated what she should and should not do. Arabelle and I agreed that women instinctively knew what would be best for an unborn child, unless there were complications, so we advised Naomi to follow her own heart.

Davey, too, wanted to help. Every morning he'd go to the

yard, picking up small branches and twigs left by the storm. He stacked them on the side porch. Later, during the icy days of December and January, we made use of them to start fires in the fireplace. The men helping Garland split up the large fallen tree after the roof was repaired. From it, we had more than ample firewood to get us through winter.

After the sun set, tired but gratified with all we'd accomplished, we enjoyed the meals Naomi prepared for us. After we ate, we sat around the fireplace making plans for Christmas. "I think on Christmas Eve we should invite all the men and women who helped us," I told my husband one evening as the fire crackled, causing shadows to dance about the room. I knew he wouldn't object. Though he never apologized for ignoring my disdain for the bed rest he ordered during my pregnancy, I suspected from such small gestures as picking up ripe persimmons and bringing them to me to make a pudding or repairing the cherished trunk that had once belonged to my mother that he wished to make amends.

He nodded. "I suppose we should have a gathering. Hard as they worked, I'm certain they'd be gratified to see the house whole and comfortable again. Perhaps we could sing Christmas carols."

Davey, a big grin splitting his face, ran to me. "Mama, can I help?"

"Certainly, we couldn't possibly do it without you."

I glanced at Naomi. Her head was bent over her needlework. Her fingers continued to cross-stitch as she lifted the needle up, then down.

Because we had a large quantity of green, yellow and white gourds of various sizes, Naomi suggested we combine them with holly berries to decorate the mantel and table. Garland chopped down a small cedar tree as we strung berries, making garlands. By Christmas Eve, all decorations were in place.

Garland opened bottles of the muscadine wine he'd made the previous summer. A large bowl of shiny apples sat on the table alongside Johnny cakes and jelly for everyone.

That evening our house rang with song as we lifted our voices singing familiar carols. Hal McCurry, who had moved with his wife Eva into Nellie's house, brought his fiddle. As he sang songs of his homeland in faraway Ireland, we tapped our feet.

Heaviness dropped from my shoulders. All thoughts of the tragedies besetting us that year drifted away. Instead, my thoughts moved to the future. Arabelle told me once again that someday I'd have a daughter with blond curly hair. If I could gather enough trust, perhaps I could make it so.

Losing children during infancy was common in our community. Women were expected to bear one baby, then another. Children were necessary to help with the farming. Other women didn't give up when they lost a child. I vowed to be brave like them. I had several child-bearing years left, so as our voices rose up in communal joy that hallowed evening, I clung to hope again.

By nine, everyone had left. Going outside with Garland, I pointed out Polaris, the brightest star in the sky.

He kissed me lightly on the lips before we went back inside and to bed.

In the middle of the night, the sound of someone moaning woke me. Intuitively, I knew. Shaking my husband's shoulders, I pleaded, "Wake up, Garland."

Finally he stirred. "What?"

"Naomi's having her baby. Go find Arabelle. Get her here quick as you can."

Nineteen

Before dawn, Arabelle burst through the door with her basket of potions, salves, herbs, and a bird's wing. "You soon be all right," she said, as she neared where Naomi sat groaning on her narrow bed.

Turning to me, she asked, "Where's clean cloths and hot water?"

How foolish I felt for the lack of preparation.

Immediately, Arabelle went to Naomi, taking her wrist to check her pulse, then lifted her dress, which revealed a stomach as large as a full-grown pumpkin.

Going downstairs to the main room, I stirred up the fire and hung a pot of water on the hook to warm. Next I took from a small box the stack of white cloths Naomi had washed for her baby's birthing.

I returned to the tiny bedroom containing only a bed, a trunk, a straight-back chair, and a mirror tacked above a table which contained some of Naomi's treasured acorns, quartz stones, and arrowheads. Arabelle's voice radiated confidence.

"Within an hour, new life will join us."

Far more skeptical, I bowed my head, pleading with God to keep death away from the house this time.

Arabelle tip-toed about the room, chanting and lighting candles. I had no idea what the words issuing from her mouth meant, but the chant calmed me. The soothing sound must have provided Naomi with tranquility as well. Tension left her face. She relaxed against the feather pillow.

"Your body be meant for birthing now that you be a full-grown woman." Arabelle smiled. "You gots wide hipbones, ample room for an infant to grow."

I bit my lip as my hands found my own hipbones, narrow, unsuitable. How I envied Naomi. How I wanted to be her, giving birth to a healthy full-term child.

Naomi writhed—her face frozen by anguish. The soft glow of candlelight didn't soften the vision. She screamed once the pain lessened.

Arabelle motioned with her hand for me to come. "Help her. Hold her hand; rub her shoulders." From her basket she removed a small tin of salve which she handed to me. With her eyes looking directly into Naomi's, she demanded, "Breathe," once the pain had passed. Naomi and I both inhaled deeply.

When the next pain washed across Naomi, she cursed. Some of the words she used, I'd never heard before. I wondered if she'd learned such crude language from her uncle. The ever recurring vision of him, his body, lifeless and cold; splotches of blood smeared on the meadow grass, came to mind. Once again, as so many times before, I wondered who killed him. Would we ever know?

Her face pale and her forehead damp with perspiration, Naomi finally closed her eyes. Dipping one of the cloths in hot water, I let it cool a bit before using it to wash her frowning face and clammy hands. Opening the tin of salve,

I applied some to Naomi's forehead. The scent of it rose up, a scent as sweet as the summer day Naomi had first come to our house as a child and chased yellow-winged butterflies about the yard. When I pushed damp strands of hair from her face, she touched my hand and moaned.

Arabelle bent down, boldly examining between Naomi's legs again. "The babe's done crowned." Her triumphant voice lifted my anxiety. "Now don't stop pushing when the next pain come."

When it came, less than a minute later, Naomi's eyes opened as wide as those of a frightened deer. Though she covered her mouth with her hand, her scream still contained all the misery of the world.

I squeezed her hand. "God will help you."

Arabelle had her head and arms between Naomi's knees again. "One more push," she said, "and you be getting the new one into the world."

Naomi's fingernails bit into the skin of my palms. "Don't quit, don't quit," I encouraged. Remaining true to her stubborn nature, she didn't.

Earlier, after bringing Arabelle to our farm, Garland had wisely escaped, Davey in tow. While Arabelle cleaned up Naomi and her baby, I left to deliver the good news. I caught sight of Davey first, then Garland, both of them near the hen stall, gathering pine cones and kindling for the fire. Hearing my footsteps, Davey ran toward me. "Mama. Mama."

He pushed his head against the soft cotton of my dress. I picked him up by his hands and swung him around until he giggled. Feeling lightheaded, I stopped. "More, more," he demanded.

Garland joined us. "How is Naomi?" Concern furrowed

his brow.

"She's fine."

"Davey pulled at my skirt. "Where have you and Omi been?"

Remember, I told you that we would get a baby sister or brother for you?"

He nodded. "Did you find my baby brother, Mama? Was he in a pumpkin shell?"

I laughed. "No, but we found you something better, a pretty little sister."

Davey frowned. "I asked for a brother."

Despite Davey's disappointment, I felt exhilarated. Even if Naomi's daughter had been my own, I'm not sure I would have been happier.

I did all within my power for Naomi and her daughter during the next few months. Though I never admitted it to myself then, I realize now that I fell into a habit of pretending her baby was my own. "What will you name the child?" I asked her several times.

For the first three weeks, she shook her head or said, "I need to think on it more," but finally, on a day when I didn't inquire, she reached for my hand when I entered her bedroom. "I've decided."

"Decided what?"

"I'm naming the child Mary."

I felt my face redden. "Did you think that was what I wanted? Mary's such an ordinary name. You can surely come up with something better. Find your daughter an interesting name; a name that will be remembered."

"I chose Mary to honor you. I thought you would be pleased."

"I am pleased, but you owe me nothing, Dear. You have

done more for me than I could ever do for you."

When she said, "How I wish that were true," her words surprised me.

After finally accepting her request, I tiptoed to the crib that had once held Davey. Tiny Mary smiled in her sleep. I wondered what she might be dreaming. Then startled, probably by my presence, she opened her eyes and whimpered. Stooping down, I touched her rosy cheeks. Gathering her in my arms, I held her close. Already, my heart had expanded providing ample room for this tiny child with golden curls. With Naomi's two children living there, beneath my roof, I felt as if I'd realized the dream I'd had since childhood, the dream to be a mother. When I lifted Mary to kiss her cheek, she frowned. I would have handed the infant to her birth mother, but Naomi had fallen asleep, so walking quietly, I took her upstairs to my own bedroom.

I looked out the window at trees bare of all leaves. For a moment or two, the sight of them reminded me of my own barren womb. Then, remembering the cycles of seasons, I envisioned the tree glorious in the spring. Perhaps my season would come someday. Perhaps I would still bear children.

Mary, even at that young age, was a quiet child. Moving her away from the light streaming through the window, I placed her on my bed. From the small pedestal table in the room, I lifted my Bible. I turned to a page near the back, titled Family Births and Deaths. The names of my parents and brothers and sisters were already there. Beneath my name and Garland's, I picked up a quill and wrote David Logan Eversole and on the next line, Mary Naomi Eversole.

Though I suffered more than a twinge of guilt for taking it upon myself to record their births, as if Naomi's children belonged to me and Garland, I nevertheless believed I was bestowing on them a favor they would need, the favor of providing a record attesting to their legitimacy.

Soon after finishing the entry and replacing the Bible back where it had been, Mary began to cry softly. Surely she was hungry. I needed to get her to Naomi. Walking over to the bed, I looked at the child, her face touched by sunlight. Her appearance startled me, particularly her pale curls and the tilt of her chin. The child surely resembled Garland. How could that possibly be?

Twenty

We seemed, I suppose, a strange family to the other Quakers living in our community. Still my closeness to Naomi and her two illegitimate children continued. Garland no longer objected. I suppose I should have wondered why, for he'd always been a conservative man clinging to what he believed acceptable. Perhaps, I decided, he didn't wish to disrupt the peaceful arrangement we currently enjoyed.

After the ground thawed in March, we had no time to sort out what should be done concerning Naomi and her children. Mouths had to be fed. All talk of feelings and the future had to be set aside to prepare the land for crops and to take up again the repairs still needed due to the damage from winter storms. Naomi volunteered for the outside chores. I looked after the children, the meals, and sewing. I also attempted a spring cleaning of all areas inside the house, but progress was slow. Always the children needed me to feed them, read them a book or teach them something new. How could I refuse? I didn't even wish to do so. Being near them provided me with more contentment than I'd ever expected to experience.

One cool day as dark clouds hovered above us, the children played their usual games as I cooked beef stew over the fire. Davey, pushing his tin soldiers aside, came to me, pulling at my long dress. "Please, Mama, tell us a story," he begged.

Mary, in the cradle I'd placed near where I worked, slept beside her corncob doll, the one I'd once given to Naomi. Waking, her face turned red; angry tears filled he eyes. "So, my children want a story. How could I deny either of you?" When I reached for Davey's hand, he resisted. "I'm a big boy, Mama." And so he was, for, according to the mark I'd made on the wall, he'd grown two inches since the previous year.

Sitting in the rocking chair by the fire, I held Mary while Davey, his legs akimbo, sat at my feet. There with them, as I watched flames lick the logs, memories of my own childhood ignited. "My mother used to tell me stories," I told the children. "She knew stories of knights and princesses and pirates. Her stories carried me to other places, other times. She also told stories of rabbits, birds, and the two cats we owned. Would you like to hear one of them?"

"Did Omie like your mother's stories?" Davey's large brown eyes, so like those of his birth mother, fastened on mine. I looked away and breathed deeply, hoping to slow my heart rate. I couldn't lie, not with him sitting there, looking at me with such trust. No, I wouldn't lie, not about that.

"I didn't know Naomi then," I said, smiling, hoping I could go on with the tale.

"Where was she?"

When I answered "Far away," he frowned, a puzzled look overtaking his sweet face.

Desperate to get past the awkward moment, I began, "There once was a toad named Hoppy because he hopped,

hopped, hopped. He hopped through the meadow, the woods, and when he reached the pond, he hopped right in. Hop, hop, hop…"

Finally Davey grinned.

"Please, Mama, may I finish the story?" Davey asked.

When I nodded, he said, "Hoppy wanted to find Omie. He wanted to hop right up on her lap and make her laugh. He looked and looked. He looked in the barn, in the meadow, and in the garden, but he couldn't find her. Not anywhere."

Wanting to say something to reassure him, I took up the thread of the story again. "Omi was also searching for Davey. She loved Davey. She wanted to play with his soldiers. She wanted to sing to him. She wanted to show him the butterflies in the meadow, the beautiful butterflies she loved to chase and catch."

Davey's sweet smile revealed two dimples, one in each of his chubby cheeks. From Mary, who had fallen asleep on my lap, came a soft snorting sound.

Play quietly, I cautioned Davey as I returned Mary to the crib. "Don't wake your little sister."

Disturbed by the yearning expressed in Davey's storytelling, I knew I should have a word with Naomi.

A few days later, she came hobbling back to the house, her arm around Arabelle's neck. She'd twisted her ankle, so wouldn't be able to work the rest of the day. After Arabelle left going back to help Garland repair a fence, I applied some of Arabelle's healing ointment and tightly wrapped strips of cloth to fortify the wound.

Naomi's thin body sagged. The dark circles beneath her eyes marred her beauty. Why did she look so pale and drawn?

"Where are the children?" she asked.

"Both are asleep, my Dear."

Realizing her injury provided an opportunity for us to talk, I took advantage.

"You work too hard," I told her.

"Hard work keeps me from thinking."

"And what do you think about, Naomi? Your beautiful children?"

"Oh, Ruthie, I don't even feel they're mine."

"Is that my fault? Though I haven't consciously tried to do so, I see now that something in me has secretly contrived to take them from you."

"They're yours, Ruthie. My gift to you, for all you've done for me and for them. As long as they're with you, I know they'll be looked after. I have nothing to give them; nothing to give anyone."

When I hugged her, I felt damp tears on her face. "We'll change this around," I said, determined not to cry.

"I ask for nothing for my children except that you continue to provide for them," she said. One corner of her mouth turned up in a grin. "But, for myself, I still long for the impossible: a husband to take care of me, a piece of land to live on, children I can publicly call my own."

How my heart ached for her. "Oh, Naomi."

Though I tried to convince her that the illegitimate births hadn't been her fault, she shook her head. When I reminded her that her uncle had forced himself on her, she rubbed her arms.

"Though I told you so, that's not quite true. He gave me trinkets for my favors. The heart-shaped necklace I used to wear, a dress, a sweet cake once."

"You were a child. How could you refuse him?"

"I was no longer a child when I conceived Mary. I knew

better, but some dark spot on my soul drove me to it anyway."

"Did you love Mary's father?"

"I suppose. I don't know," she said, looking away from me.

Then the answer was before me, clear as if written on the wall. I suppose I'd known since I first glimpsed Mary's blonde curls. No one had hair like that, no one except my husband.

"So Garland is Mary's father."

She didn't lie. She didn't turn away. Her lower lip quivered as she looked up at me. "I'll leave."

Mixed emotions tumbled inside of me. I both loved and hated her in that moment. Though I despised Naomi for stealing my husband, I couldn't imagine our household without her. Only one thing would help. I needed to get away. "Feed the children when they wake," I instructed. Rushing outside, I headed toward the river.

Twenty-One

The Deep River flowing alongside our community remained a constant in both good and bad times. I suppose that's why I suddenly yearned to go there. Too many changes were occurring. How could I survive so much turmoil? Did Garland love Naomi? Did he love me? How could someone who claimed to walk in the path of righteousness have been so misled?

I didn't know. I didn't even want to know. I could think of no explanation from either Garland or Naomi that would make everything right again.

We'd had rain the night before, so the river was wide, swollen. Water crashed and splattered over large rocks. For a while, the river tempted me with its beauty, its wildness. How easy it would be to walk in, going so far out I couldn't return. The water would eliminate all hurt, all feeling. I would be free. How I longed for such release. If I died, I would have to make no decision; I'd have to find no way to sort out the messiness.

Visions of Naomi's children floated through my mind. How could I leave Davey or Mary? Hadn't I obstinately willed them to be my own? How would they adjust to Naomi?

When I heard footsteps behind me, I turned. Naomi stood there without shoes or a shawl covering her arms. Her hair was a mess of tangles. She resembled the gypsies who had once showed up at our door, holding their hand out for coins and food.

"Come home, Ruthie," she begged. "Just tell me what you wish me to do, and I'll do it. We all need you. You're the one our lives revolve around. Without you, the family would fall apart."

I held my tongue though I felt tempted to shout out, calling her a fallen women or those rougher words, the words men use to debase women, but there were no words to sufficiently express my disappointment in her, in Garland, even myself. Still what was I to do? The light within, the light I'd depended on to guide me, had been blown out by those I loved. I couldn't seek help among my Quaker sisters. To do so would destroy Garland's reputation. Only one person could help. "Naomi, go see to your children. I'll be back by suppertime."

"I'm worried about you."

"I need some time alone."

"Will you promise to do no harm to yourself?"

"Oh, Naomi, of course I won't. Trust me."

How surprised I was when she reached out, hugging me.

"Go now," I said sternly. "The children need you."

Reluctantly, she turned. After waiting long enough for her to reach the farmhouse, I left the river, walking down a path I'd never taken before. As I walked at least half a mile, the sun disappeared behind a cloud. Though my heart beat rapidly, I kept my eyes on the rough path until I spotted a row of shanty houses, barely strong enough to stand. Red peppers hung on one door. That must be Arabelle's place, I decided. She often spoke of hot peppers keeping trouble away.

When she answered my knock, the look on her face let me know she'd been expecting me. I fell into her arms and sobbed until there were no more tears. She pulled me inside. Turning to her smiling children, she asked them to go outside so we could talk. I sat in a cane chair and looked around. Colorful drawings hung on the walls. There were also painted gourds and crosses made of sticks, leaves and pieces of straw.

"Naomi and Garland..." I began.

"I know," she said, her eyes brown pools of understanding.

"Why did no one tell me?"

"I can't speak for others, but I couldn't bear to break your heart?"

Feeling empty and useless, I stared at Arabelle, hoping to absorb her calm demeanor. I couldn't keep my hands still; though I interlaced my fingers, they still shook.

What am I to do?"

"What we all do, Mary Ruth. Live til angels take us away. Live for the children. Live for Garland and Naomi."

Anger, hot as fire, suddenly flamed inside me. Glaring at Arabelle, I demanded, "Put a hex on Garland and Naomi. Make them suffer."

Laughter issued from her, a sound so large it filled every corner of the shanty. "What I practice is Hoodoo, not voodoo."

"They need to be punished."

"They has been. I certain of it."

When I asked if I should force Naomi to leave, perhaps even leave myself, she said, "Where would you go?"

I stood, pacing back and forth in the small space, grieving my predicament, wondering how I could endure the awkwardness of living with my husband and his mistress. For the longest time, Arabelle sat quietly, saying nothing. Finally, she spoke, helping me understand. "Mr. Eversole fail cause he try too hard not to. Always following a straight path not be possible, especially for men. We not meant to be perfect. We all flawed. I learn the truth of it through my own birth. The slave owner on the plantation where I once be decided to be kind to my mother. He bring her apples and taught her to read. Soon he found his way between her legs. That where I come from."

Tears glistened on Arabelle's cheeks.

"Oh, Arabelle. I never knew. I never even thought…"

"You never notice that my skin be the color of wet sand, not black?"

As late afternoon sunlight filtered through the open door of Arabelle's house, I looked at my once beautiful hands, which had become rough and red from work. I scrunched up my fingers to hide the dirt beneath my nails. Why couldn't we keep clean? Catching the scent of myself, sweat mingled with fear, I placed my hand over my nose, hoping to escape the stink of my own self.

I closed my eyes and spoke, telling a story from long ago, a story passed down from generation to generation in my mother's family. "There was once a boy named Icarus. His father made him wings of wax. Soon Icarus could fly anywhere he wished to go, but he foolishly flew too high. When he touched the sun, his wings caught fire and melted. Icarus tumbled to the ground."

Arabelle nodded her head. Turning, she spit a black stream of tobacco into the fire.

Had the flight Garland and I made to this new place been too ambitious? Was that the reason we'd been burned? Had Naomi lured Garland or had he forced himself on her. I shook my head, unable to envision it either way. But I would have to find out. How could I live without knowing?

"Blame everyone and no one," Arabelle said, as if reading my mind.

"Blaming no one is impossible." Anger rose in my throat. I felt as if bands bound my shoulders and chest. I attempted to breathe deeply but could not.

"You are strong, Mary Ruth, stronger than you know. You will forgive. You will do it for the children. It be time to go home and settle your soul."

"Come with me." Tears streamed down my face and hers.

"You must go alone. I ain't got no magic for this. It up to you to make peace or not."

"I'm frightened, Arabelle."

"There be a full moon tonight. It light your way. There also be that light inside you talks about so much. Surely it will help, too."

"It's no longer there. Nothing's there."

"The light still burn. Go home, rest yourself, then you see it again."

Twenty-Two

When I arrived home, I lifted the kettle of water hanging above the fire. Pouring a bit of it into the cup that had belonged to my mother, I mixed in the tea leaves Arabelle had insisted I take home with me. "The tea will help you sleep," she instructed. "Your dreams will tell you all you need to know."

The narrow steps creaked as I walked up to reach my bedroom. Once inside, I sat my cup on the table and slid the wooden peg into the lock position. That night I intended to deal with no one except my own tortured soul, but before I finished my tea, guilt raised its demanding head reminding me of duty. No use making a scene over the locked door, I decided, so finding paper and a pen, I wrote a hasty note to Garland and Naomi, letting them know that I needed time alone. I ended with, "Garland, we'll talk tomorrow." Even before I slipped the note beneath the door, exhaustion smothered my anger. I was already yawning.

Moonlight filled the room as I threw back the bed cover.

Noticing my opened Bible on the bedside table, I picked it up. Looking down, I read, "Your people shall be my people." Had Naomi left it there, hoping I would find it? So weary I couldn't think clearly, my head welcomed the softness of my feather pillow. Sleep must have enveloped me quickly, for I remember nothing else of that night, nothing except the promised dream.

I dreamed of the second little girl I'd lost. Holding her in my arms, sadness rolled over me, but I refused to let her go. Garland attempted to take the dead child from me, but I screamed, and then ran until out of breath. As I leaned against the chestnut tree, struggling to recover, the baby disappeared from my arms and suddenly Davey was there, his sweet face looking up at me, calling me "Mama." He shook one of the lower limbs of the tree and magically, apples instead of chestnuts fell around us—dozens of them, red and ripe. Picking up the largest one, he rushed over, handing it to me. And then Sweet little Mary, her yellow curls all a mess, was there with us, too, laughing, rolling down a hill.

The next morning, I still recalled the curious details of the strange dream, including how both children began chasing one of the young pigs. Davey finally caught onto it, but the piglet slipped from his arms. Then Mary fell on the pig's back and all of us laughed. Petite Mary trapping the pig with her tiny body became the funniest thing we had ever seen. Our laughter rang out so loudly across the meadow, it awakened me.

Despite the heartbreak of the day before, I sat up in bed, a smile on my face. Still uncertain what I must do, I knew with great certainly what I wouldn't do. Under no circumstances would I desert those children. Though not mine by blood, they were mine by love, and I intended having them no matter what price I might have to pay for the privilege.

Before I had time to dress and plan my day, I heard the two of them outside the bedroom door. "Shh," I heard Davey say to his little sister.

"I need Mama," Mary countered.

"Papa said we should not disturb her. She needs to rest."

"Mama sick?"

"I don't think so," Davey answered.

"Then I need to see her now."

I easily imagined how Mary might look. Her lower lip would be stuck out. She'd stomp her tiny foot. How could I deny either of them entry.

Dressing quickly I opened the door. With my hands on my hips, I looked down at Mary. "Well, who knocked over your pony cart?" I asked. "If you're not careful, little lady, you'll trip right over that lip." Reaching out I tousled her hair. Davey, forcing himself between the two of us, fiercely grabbed hold of my legs.

"If you promise to be very good, you can come inside my bedroom. As soon as I wash my face, I'll tell you a story about a brave little girl who captured a pig."

Twenty-Three

Though Garland surely realized I knew of his relationship with Naomi, I never accused him directly. Avoiding him was easy. As the farm grew, we became busier and busier. We prospered during the next months in many ways. We were able to live comfortably and added a shed near the house for the chickens.

Encouraged by Arabelle, we found an additional use for the building. Slaves had begun escaping to the North during those perilous times. We helped as many of those as we could by allowing them to share space with the hens for a few days. Though Garland appeared concerned when I first suggested the idea, he allowed it without protesting. We soon aided over twenty of them who dreamed of eventually reaching Canada where, hopefully, they would be offered an olive branch of freedom.

I once asked Arabelle, "Wouldn't you like to go across the border and take your children?"

"If younger, yes," she answered honestly, "but now I be

too old for adventures." Perhaps someday the children will go, savoring the sweetness of freedom. But it'll be only a taste. People always be taking advantage of others long as they get by with it. One hundred years backward or one hundred forward, I spect it be the same."

Though pleased to be offered a nugget of truth, I sighed, hoping to relieve some of the heaviness her answer caused me. "Ah, yes, tis a human flaw, I fear, to take advantage of others. Sometimes I worry that I take advantage of you, Arabelle. And Naomi, have I taken advantage of her as well?"

"Taking advantage be equal between you and Naomi. As for myself, nobody take advantage of Arabelle. I makes sure of that."

During the following months, Naomi's behavior troubled me. Had her unbridled delight charmed Garland? And was their attraction, like dust in a house, impossible to sweep away? To my mind, the mischief of my husband and Naomi still clung to the walls as if glued on. Yet outwardly, I remained civil, never daring to ask "Why?" the question that most worried my heart.

One afternoon, as October sunlight became a thin orange line in the west, I walked outside the house and offered a solution to my husband. "Build a small place for Naomi," I suggested, "one large enough for her clothes and a bed. She can stay there, and you can stay in her old room downstairs. I no longer wish my home to be hers. I no longer wish to have you in my bed."

I didn't expect him to agree, but looking down, as if giving serious thought to the red clay covering his boots, he nodded.

Yellow, purple and red tree leaves flamed that fall. In contrast, a part of me became dormant. Tucked away from pain, I felt empty but not useless. I could work and did. I dried all manner of fruit and vegetables. I made a new quilt, one for my own bed. On it, I embroidered the faces of children. Their presence would warm me during chilly evenings. They would not forsake me and hopefully neither would Naomi's children. If they did, how would I survive?

Naomi gave up the yellow apron she loved. Now, like me, she usually wore pale brown or washed-out blue. Still, unlike other women in our community, she failed to cover her head with a square of cloth unless I demanded it, and though I provided her a bonnet to wear in public, she sometimes left it at home.

Naomi's frequent laughter remained as before, loud and free. Still whatever I bid her do, she did without complaint. One day, she returned early from the field. Looking away from me, she begged for my forgiveness. "I considered you my sister," she said. "You taught me most of what I know. I shouldn't have failed you."

My heart hardened despite her seeming sincerity. I allowed her to be there near my husband and her children, but I could not, would not relinquish more. A heart, even the heart of a dedicated Quaker woman, is capable of withstanding just so much harm and hurt, without breaking. At least, that's what I believed then.

We celebrated Mary's third birthday on a windswept day. The child, a little enchantress even then, turned in circles while Davey, like a little man, examined the clouds, asking Garland, "Do you think bad weather's blowing in? Don't you think the animals need to be inside the barn?"

Garland looked up, sniffed the air, then leaned nearer Davey, patting his head. "You might be right. Want to help?"

As the two of them walked off hand in hand, I watched

little Mary stuff her tiny mouth with blackberries. Dark juice ran down her chin. Naomi laughed, but I attempted to hide my smile behind my hand, not wishing to embarrass the child.

In seconds the sun ducked behind a cloud; the yard grew dark as dusk. Hearing the sound of a horse's hooves, I looked out to the road. At first I didn't recognize the man approaching. Extremely tall, a hat covered his hair. A mustache, large as a full-grown woolly worm grew above his upper lip; a cigar protruded from his mouth.

Once I spotted his piercing brown eyes, I knew—Jonathan Lewis, the man from across the river, the man who nearly four years before followed Naomi from a church meeting; the man I had, at first, foolishly decided was Mary's father.

He directed his gaze toward Naomi as he pulled the reins, sharply stopping his horse. "This must be the Eversole Farm," he said.

Naomi lowered her head.

"Well, it's a mighty fine place." he turned to me, touching the brim of his hat.

"We've done well," I said.

"Mrs. Eversole, my name is Jonathan, Jonathan Lewis. Might this be your daughter?"

When he grinned, smoke escaped his mouth. I cared not for the look of him nor for the overpowering smell of his cigar.

As I stood there, trying to come up with the right words, Naomi looked up at him, her chin lifted. "I'm Naomi Wise. We've met before. I'm an orphan, as you may recall, belonging to no one. The Eversoles have kindly afforded me employment."

"I see," he said, placing the hat back on his head. "Well, nice to meet you folks. Rain's coming this way. I best get home ahead of it."

"Stop by when you have more time," I said. Later, I deeply regretted speaking those simple words. Though, all of us had suffered enormous losses before, none of our previous misfortunes would compare with the damage wrought by this man with an oily grin.

Arabelle once spoke to me of ruffians who possessed an evil eye. Could the sly look directed at Naomi have been an evil eye intending her harm? If so, was there any way I could have protected her?

A loud clap of thunder startled me. Jonathan's horse rose up on its back legs, neighing. I backed away. He held the horse firmly, else I would have been killed. As the black steed turned, galloping away, a cloud of dust rose up stifling me.

Garland soon returned with Davey. His voice, sounding thin and far away, warned, "A storm's surely brewing. I can smell it. Mary Ruth, get everyone inside."

Before I reached the children, rain pelted my head. After grabbing their hands, I watched a huge elm tree being ripped from the earth, its roots exposed, naked. How could mere wind manage such a task?

"Naomi," I called.

"I'll go help, Mr. Eversole," she answered.

"No," I screamed at her, "Get inside. Protect the children."

Though my heart pounded, the storm fascinated me. The energy and intensity of the swirling leaves bore witness to the power of God. I was determined to stay outside. It was more than a sense of duty driving me to find and help my husband, for suddenly, despite his betrayal, I realized I still loved him.

As I took off running toward the field, I chided myself for acting like a child. You're worse than Naomi, I thought. Still

I ran on, calling, "Garland, where are you?"

It was a miracle I found him. He was down on the ground behind the shelter where the chickens lay their eggs. His face was smeared with blood. At first, I believed him to be unconscious, but as I pressed the bottom of my dress to his face, hoping to staunch the flow of blood, he stirred. "Mary Ruth," he said. His clammy hand touched my face. "You came for me."

The wind grabbed leaves from trees swirling them around as if they were the contents of a witch's cauldron. One evergreen and then another crackled, then fell to the ground. Such a mess. That brief thought twirled through my mind, and then I was again bent over my husband. I touched his arms and legs, checking to determine if there might be other injuries. There seemed to be none. "Do you think you can walk?" I asked. "We need to get you back."

He grimaced, but slowly sat up. With my help, he managed to finally stand, though he complained of being lightheaded. As he leaned back against the trunk of an oak tree, I found a small tree limb he could use for a cane. Together, we slowly made our way home.

It was indeed a miracle that we got through for tree branches and leaves covered the pathway. The rain and wind appeared to be carrying on a competition to determine which might do the most damage. Not until later did I concern myself with the the destruction to crops, animals, and property. All of my thoughts remained focused on Garland: getting him safely inside and willing his wounds to heal.

Not until we entered the cabin did I realize I, too, was hurt. The bodice of my dress was torn, exposing my left breast. When I covered it with my hand, I felt warm blood pulsing out of me. Picking up the quilt Naomi made, I put it around my shoulders, pretending nothing was wrong.

"Naomi," I called out. When she came to us, pale and round-eyed with fright, I told her to warm soup to eat. "And check the house, making sure the doors, windows and roof are secure. Until the storm subsides, there's nothing we can do to help the animals."

Without explaining Garland's wounds or my own, I led my husband up the stairs to my bed. Once there I poured water from the pitcher into the washbowl to clean his wounds, then after making certain the bleeding from the side of his head had clotted, I massaged Arabelle's smelly healing salve into his tortured skin. When I covered him with the quilt embroidered with the faces of children, he closed his eyes. "I don't deserve..." he began, then spoke no farther.

As he rested I stepped out of my bloody dress and cleaned my own wound. When I turned, I saw that he watched me. "How beautiful you are," he said.

I spoke plainly, honestly. "I've never thought myself so."

"Tis my fault; I've kept it from you."

How curious, I thought, but his reply opened me to him in a way I'd never been opened before. I forgot the pain of my wound, and his. After latching the door, I studied my husband for a moment, from head to foot, before helping him remove his boots and pants. What a grand creation the human body is, I thought, as he lifted my shift. Then I, too, was beneath the quilt. Perhaps the pain of our wounds added to the pleasure of our comingling that evening. Despite all my grievances against him, I'd never felt closer, neither before or since. Is this what he'd found with Naomi? I wondered, before sending the intrusive thought flying like a lost bird, hoping it would never return.

My husband kissed me and breathed deeply, as if inhaling my very essence. When the climatic moment came, joy, warm as rays of sunlight, spread through every fiber of my being.

I slept then and so did he. Later, after the storm settled to a gentle rain, Naomi knocked at my bedroom door. "Soup's ready," she said.

"Feed the children," I instructed. "Garland and I will be down later."

As my husband continued to sleep, I touched his hair; my fingers gently brushed it out of his eyes. For the first time, I noticed gray hairs intertwined with the golden strands. I smiled, and then doubt pinched my heart. Would I be with him long enough for his hair to become completely gray? Different as we were, would we be able to endure one another?

Twenty-Four

Farm life is often brutal. As a child in Pennsylvania, my days were easy compared to those I spent here in North Carolina.

My father had been a tradesman with his own shop. There he sold all manner of goods. My mother made my sister and me beautiful clothes from the cloth and yarn my father kept in his store. He also kept feed for horses, chickens and cows as well as necessities for building houses: hammers, nails, saws. The boots and shoes he sold were well known for their endurance. Without his shop, there probably would have been little music in the town of Lilith where we lived. Two or three banjos always hung on the wall alongside fiddles or as we called them, violins. Once a pipe organ took up considerable space in the middle of the store. Another time he ordered pure silk from China, so Felicia Dunworthy could have fancy drapes made for her drawing room. Whatever townspeople desired, it seemed, my father could procure it for a price.

The price we paid as a family was his neglect, never intentional, but he always needed to be at the shop or out looking for new goods. Mother consoled us in his absence, hugging us, feathering our faces with little kisses and reading stories. Though we dreaded her doses of a repugnant tonic when we had croup, we willingly opened our mouths trusting her potion to provide a quick recovery.

There were frequent parties in Pennsylvania, particularly at the Dunworthy home. We were not invited to every gathering, but our names always remained on the guest list for the Christmas dance. That's the event I loved best. One year mother made me a lavender dress. That night I danced with every young man who asked me.

But the young gentleman who most attracted me, a tall blond stranger, never requested a turn around the floor that evening. He laughed when I asked why he wasn't dancing. "My feet won't do what my mind tells them to," he answered.

"Umm," I said. Though I didn't tell him so, I understood. Dancing is letting go. The mind needs to be lost in the shuffle, so to speak. The body takes over knowing what it was never actually taught.

"Would you like some punch?" The young man asked.

"What I would truly like it to know your name."

That's how I first met Garland. Later, when he came to my house, he talked frequently of the Quakers and their desire to work for the freedom of all men, including Negroes.

Mother was interested. She asked questions, adding that she, too, would like to lighten the load of our darker brothers. "But how about women?" she added. Don't they deserve freedom as well, to vote, to own land?"

My father, who usually had little to say during such conversations, took the cigar from his mouth long enough to sputter, "Hell, no."

"Why, pray tell?" Mother asked.

My father gulped down the rest of his brandy, then smoothed down the corners of his ample mustache. "Order would be destroyed. Nature has a design. Some are meant to make the rules. Others, including women, need to follow."

My mother's pretty face sagged.

Remembering that conversation between my parents always reminded me why I left my comfortable life in Pennsylvania. I suppose I thought women would have freedom in the Utopia Garland described. Although our journey from Pennsylvania was a most arduous undertaking, I felt so alive during those days and nights. I trusted my husband completely then.

Once a huge black bear came within six feet of us. I had no notion what to do, nor did Garland. Finally, inhaling deeply, I began dancing an Irish jig, moving backwards with each step. At first the bear moved side to side as well, as if imitating my movements. Finally, when I'd danced away and Garland had moved some distance from him, the bear turned, waddling toward a thick groove of trees.

I remember trembling. Garland reached out holding me. During those minutes, I resolved to be a good Quaker, and successfully did so for years after our treacherous journey ended. Actually until the day I neglected Nellie by forsaking her, letting her die alone.

Hadn't Nellie warned me about the ophan and her people? Hadn't Garland foreseen the disaster that might result with her under our roof?

Mule-headed, I'd listened to no one.

Arabelle joined us the day after the storm. I welcomed her with open disbelieving arms. Were her children all right? I wanted to know. How about the place where she dwelled, only a tiny shanty that might have easily blown away?

Her wide grin assured me all was fine. Pulling away from me, she examined the scratches on my body. After Garland kissed my cheek, he said, "I'd best get outside and begin mending what might be saved."

After he left, Arabelle's eyebrows arched like miniature rainbows. "Ah, something's been mended here" she said. Feeling the warmth of a blush suffuse my face, I lowered my head. My friend laughed loudly.

She touched my cheek with her warm hand. Then speaking softly, she declared, "May angels be praised. Was it you or Mr. Eversole who managed the thaw?" Taking out some new ointment from her basket, one that smelled worse than bog water, she coated her finger with it, touching my scratches. "Show me the worse wound," she requested. When I unbuttoned my bodice, she sucked in a great gulp of air.

"Arabelle, it's all right," I tried convincing her, though my entire breast was a purple bruise. "What does it matter, anyway? A breast is of little use to me. I'll never suckle a child."

She pursed her lips. "Such as that not be for you to know. It up to a higher power, so if you be wise, you'll leave it that way. Otherwise worrying will eat up your mind."

"Me? It's you who are always predicting this and that. How many of your predictions actually come true?"

"All of them." she said, raising her chin.

I looked her in the eye, feeling sure she'd back down. When she only sniffed in a haughty manner as if secrets could be inhaled, I reminded her she'd told me twice I'd have a girl child. "All lies," I said.

"No, not lies. It will happen. You will see. My predictions don't fail, I fail. Though I know the event, I don't always get the timing right."

There was too much to do to stand there arguing, so I recited a list of what I knew needed to be done inside the house and yard. "Before you begin, go check with Garland. I'm sure the greatest damage is beyond the house. See to whatever he needs first. Naomi can help me here."

When she turned to walk away, I hurried to her, encircling her from behind with my arms. "Forgive me for doubting you. Without you knowledge and strong back, we wouldn't survive."

"Make peace with Naomi," she answered. "You need her too."

Twenty-Five

I delayed speaking to Naomi until I could avoid it no more. At first, I made the excuse that we were both too busy for conversation. Then I convinced myself it was not my business to interfere with her life. Hadn't I initially made such a mistake and hadn't it brought a storm down on our household even more destructive than the recent natural storm which had attacked our property. Yet, try as I might to separate myself from her, I couldn't. Our lives had become linked, though not in the foolish idealistic way I'd imagined more than eight years ago when I'd shared with her the story of Ruth and Naomi from the Bible. How much we differed from those two. Though I couldn't speak for the orphan, I'd never in my heart sincerely pursued a path of "Whither thou goest, I will go," following her. No, my way had been to convince her to go my way and when she had not, refusing to behave in a respectable manner, I no longer empathized.

Still we remained oddly intertwined, like two different plants, their separate vines twined around one another. Even

Arabelle made mention of the invisible bond between us.

Though not a good time to do so, considering all the work that needed to be done, I went for a walk to clear my head. I soon found myself at the river. Since the storm, the banks had flooded and overrun. Wind had wrestled limbs from trees and the shore line now stretched in at least a foot from where it had been before. Overhead, the sky was blue again, the air clean. Grateful, I inhaled deeply until my mind grew quiet, then after meditating, I turned to walk home.

Determined to speak to Naomi before Garland and Arabelle returned, I found her bending over a pot of stew as it cooked over the fire. "Come with me," I demanded, "Let's go upstairs."

As she followed me, I fancied I heard her heart beating. Probably, it was my own.

Once in the room, I bid her sit, pointing to the straight back chair. "If we are to continue together here," I said, standing above her, "there are limits that must be adhered to. As we know, you've already birthed two illegitimate children, both lovely, both loved by my husband and me. I believe and you haven't denied that the oldest was fathered by your uncle. How lucky we are that nothing seems to be wrong with him, except one eye that turns slightly inward. As I'm sure you know, cross breeding can do ruinous harm to a child."

I'd never seen Naomi sit so still. To remain quiet conflicted with her usual demeanor. Her face paled as I continued to talk. Except for the slightest lifting and falling of her bosom, I wouldn't have been certain the poor girl was breathing.

"Your second child, our Mary was, as you've admitted, fathered by my own husband. I will never ask again if you went to him or he came to you. But I will tell you that if it ever happens again, I will kill you both."

I wasn't certain where such violent words came from.

Naomi's head jerked up; her eyes were pools of disbelief. She made not one sound, but tears flowed down her face. I wanted her to share my hurt. If she'd been a child still, I would have shaken her. A horrible memory suddenly filled my head. My father, his strong hands on my shoulders, pumping them back and forth, shouting at me, "I'll shake some sense into your head, young lady."

Yes, if only I could shake sense into Naomi's head. That's all I wished to do. Make her see as I saw. Make her see what she must avoid.

Suddenly, for no clear reason, I went to Naomi, hugging her to me. "What I'm saying is meant for your own good. You can't have my husband. I've welcomed him back to my bed."

After brushing tears away with her sleeves, Naomi stepped back and stared at me as if I were an enemy. "I don't want your husband," she said. "I've even willingly given up my own children. But I must have something, don't you see?"

"Jonathan Lewis? Is that what you want, Naomi? Well, you can't have him and it won't be my fault. You are an orphan, an orphan with two illegitimate children. The world we live in is not fair, particularly to women. He doesn't want to marry you. He simply wants to use you."

"What if I leave here?"

"Without your children?"

"What if I take the children?"

Davey came bursting through the door running toward me. I grabbed and hugged him. "Precious boy," I said, then with a corner of my apron wiped the hot tears that came coursing down my face and neck. Eventually the salt of them reached my breast, causing my wound to sting.

"You will never take these children away," I said to Naomi, speaking over the boy's head, "for you have never made them yours."

Twenty-Six

I talked to Garland that day, then the two of us met with Naomi. If she would stay and continue to help us on the farm, he would build a one-room cabin for her on the Western edge of our property line. The children would remain in the big house with us, but she could be with them whenever she wanted. In exchange, she would do as she did now, helping maintain our home, the herb garden, and tending the animals.

She smiled stiffly.

"I've never meant to harm you," I said. "I'd hoped that I could help."

"You can never make another person's life what you wish it to be." She spoke so softly, I had difficulty comprehending the words. I looked at her for a long moment before nodding agreement. If I could only go back, things might be different, I thought. "If only, if only" words so futile they never deserve utterance.

After our conversation, a new pattern emerged. Naomi avoided us except to work, and her hours were more regular now. At her own suggestion, she worked from dawn until two hours before dusk. She prepared the morning meal for us, but ate before we sat at the table. She also prepared the big meal in late afternoon and cleaned up, taking leftovers home for herself. If she had time, she spent it on needlework, making a quilt or curtains to cover the one window in her own place.

"I miss Naomi," Arabelle said to me one afternoon.

"Yes, I do too," I confessed.

"I suppose it be good. She now have a life of her own."

Though I never visited Naomi in her own place, I noticed that Arabelle sometimes did. When I asked her about it, she said, "That girl gonna need protection. I helps her out with a some of my hoodoo."

Naomi still owned Sadie, the horse Garland gave her. On Sundays, she didn't work, but she no longer attended Friends' monthly meetings or other gatherings. Whenever our family returned from the meeting house, both Naomi and the horse would be gone. At one meeting, Etta Fields, told me what I already suspected: "Naomi's been seen with that man from across the river."

I never asked which one. I didn't have to. When I told Garland, he appeared deeply disturbed, his head down, his fingers rubbing his forehead as if what was to come could be rubbed away. "What is it you want from me, Mary Ruth?"

"Save her."

"Shall I chain her to a fence post?"

"Of course not."

Because neither of us could come up with a solution, I

sought Arabelle's advice. She, too, was at a loss. But she agreed that we must do something, so slowly, over the next few days, we devised a plan. Arabelle tried secret spells to protect Naomi. I tried words. Whenever, I had a few moments, I'd write down a Bible verse or a quotation I'd heard, and then later, while Naomi was working at our house, I'd hurry to her humble home and slip written messages beneath her door.

Once, peeking inside the window, I saw how pretty Naomi had made her place. Red berries in a glass bowl sat on the table, alongside a jar of pretty river rocks. On her walls were black and white sketches of flowers, trees, and one large portrait of a man. When I looked closely, I realized it was Jonathan.

One morning, soon after the first breath of spring blew through Randolph County, I woke feeling puny. Garland must have noticed, for he insisted on carrying me down the stairs. The hoe cakes Naomi fixed for our breakfast were already on the table. Just the smell of them made my stomach lurch. Garland urged me to spend the day in bed.

"But there's so much to be done," I protested. The icy feel of winter had finally left as a few flourishes of spring began inhabiting our land again. Try as we might, with so many storms both inside our house and outside, we were barely breaking even. If this year turned out be a good one, we could begin to have more for our children than clothes for their backs and food on the table. Hopefully, we'd even have more we could share with Arabelle and Naomi. They, too, would profit from a good year. Still, as I sat there, even the smell of coffee, which I usually found invigorating, made me ill.

Managing to smile despite the discomfort, I placed a hoe cake on my plate and took a tiny bite. Garland touched my hand. When he placed strips of hog meat on his plate, I stood up and hurried from the room. Just as I rushed from the house, Arabelle walked up, a basket balanced on her head. "Uh-oh," she said, soon as she saw the expression on my face. After walking past her to weeds growing nearby, I gave up the contents of my stomach. Swiftly, she followed, one arm around my waist, the other one touching my forehead.

"Don't tell, Garland," I begged.

"There already be so many secrets clouding this house, I can't see straight. Mary Ruth, you gots to get those secrets cleared away fore your can move on."

"I'm going to bed," I said. "Bad dreams kept interrupting my sleep last night."

Turning me around, her dark eyes studied me for what seemed like the longest time. "Not sleeping has nothing to do with your sick belly. You been through it before. Surely, you recognize what it be."

"Impossible," I said.

"Only if your husband ain't been in your bed. Otherwise, it surely be."

"Help me, Arabelle," I said. "I need to get upstairs to my bedroom without upsetting Garland."

"Since it be half his doing, he ought to be at least half upset."

When I glanced up, Garland came through the door. Slowly, I moved away to a spot away from the weeds. "Mary Ruth, are you all right?" he asked.

"I'm fine," I said. "I just came out to meet Arabelle. I need her to stay at the house. I have some things I need looking after today."

Though he looked at me for a long while, as if waiting for an explanation, he finally turned away. Since I'd discover his mischief with Naomi, he no longer objected to any of my suggestions. Patting me on the shoulder before leaving for the fields, he looked toward Arabelle. "Call me if I'm needed."

Arabelle washed my face and hands with a clean cloth once she had me in the bedroom.

"Tell me how to get rid of this baby growing inside me," I said. "I can't bare to lose another one. I don't have the time to stay in bed, being careful. Wishing for a healthy child will again prove futile."

"Only God knows what's going to be."

When I turned over sobbing, she rubbed my back. "Being abed during the last pregnancies didn't work for you. Maybe this time, you should stay up."

"Garland will never allow it."

"Perhaps, he won't puzzle out what's happening, at least not for a while." When she smiled, I noticed she'd lost another tooth. "Though I don't usually prescribe secrets, maybe one's needed just this once."

"I'll need help," I said.

"I be right here," she said. "I mix up something for your sickness and when you feel real bad, we'll tell Garland you need fresh air."

"It'll never work. What about Naomi? Won't she suspect?"

"Maybe she be too concerned about herself for thoughts of others to creep in."

That afternoon, Arabelle gave me a bitter potion to settle my stomach. Then we laid our plans. When I didn't feel well I'd cough and she'd tell Garland I needed to be upstairs so the children wouldn't take sick too.

During the next two months, we rarely resorted to deception. Keeping to my usual schedule, I rarely had a bad spell. Indeed I remained so hearty that a bubble of hope began to rise inside of me. Perhaps, I would finally have a child of my own. Arabelle seemed to believe it. Why shouldn't I?

Twenty-Seven

Not more than a month later, coinciding with the advent of spring, Naomi began behaving more like her old self. When the wind blew, she'd turn around and around, often holding either Davey or Mary by their hands. Her laughter rang out across the meadow. Sometimes, entertaining the children, she also make chirping sounds, imitating a cardinal, and lured other winged creatures into conversations only she could understand. When she helped the children find an owl at dusk, Davey answered the round-eyed creature's hoot with a hoot of his own. How the children loved her when she became one of them, exploring the ground for interesting stones and arrowheads and telling stories of magical creatures that both frightened and delighted them.

That evening as we prepared for bed, the children already sleeping soundly in the room below, Garland lamented that Naomi had been neglecting some of her chores.

"She's been spending more time with the children. Isn't

that more important?"

"Why is it that you always defend her, Mary Ruth? For us, the children and the community, nothing can be more important than a good crop." His words cut like the blade of a knife. As he looked out our bedroom window, I stood on the tips of my toes and peered over his shoulder. The moon, full and glorious, lit up the nighttime sky. When Garland turned, I noticed worry wrinkles creasing his forehead.

"The truth, Garland, is that I'm expecting a child and if this pregnancy, like all the others, goes sour, I might not live to look after Davey and Mary. If that happens, how will we manage without Naomi?"

He looked at me with such tenderness. Quickly moving to where I stood, he took my face in his hands. "Why didn't you tell me? I'm going to get the doctor to come," he said. "I'll ride over to Asheboro in the morning."

"No, Garland. Following the doctors' orders didn't work the last time, so I'll have none of him now. Arabelle will help, and Naomi."

Clenching his jaw, he held me so tightly it became uncomfortable. When I pulled away, he finally let go.

"In most households men make decisions. Don't you think that's what God intends?"

"What I think Garland if that God intends men to remain faithful to their wives." I placed my hand on my stomach. "I want what's best for the child inside of me. A life-giving cord connects us. Shouldn't that afford me and our child some rights?"

"You know nothing of medicine."

"No, but Arabelle does. I intend to place my faith totally in her this time."

Frowning, he sat on the bed and stared at his boots. "Nothing is as I imagined it might be. Not any more. So much is changing in the world. So much has changed between you and me."

Sitting down beside him, I touched his knee. "There's always been change. There always will be. I'm going to pick blackberries with Arabelle tomorrow. How about I make you a pie? Think that might make you feel better?"

He managed a small smile. "Well, blackberry pie never hurt a soul that I've heard about."

The next morning I spoke to Naomi as I reached for the basket and washing pan Arabelle and I would need for berries. "Stay here with the children," I said.

"What about Mr. Eversole?" she asked. "He said he needed me to be in the fields."

"I've informed my husband that I'd be asking you to stay. Look after Davey and Mary. Arabelle and I will be back by noon."

Reaching out, I drew her to me, remembering how once I'd considered her my daughter, not by blood, but of my heart. When I said, "I trust you," she pulled away from me.

Once in the woods, I relaxed. Everything was soft, fresh. The mingled smells of earth and flora lifted my spirit. Arabelle insisted I lay down on the pine-needled path to rest a bit. Sitting beside me, she circled her large hands in front of my body again and again. When I inquired what she doing, she replied. "I be drawing all poisons out of you."

Foolish as the words sounded, I embraced them. Above the sky was blue and cloudless. I knew it would be a day I'd always remember. The walk had awakened my spirit. The taste of warm blackberries excited my tongue. "The world would be so much better," I said to Arabelle, "if everyone spent more time out-of-doors."

"That be the truth," she said. "Yes, that be the blessed

truth."

On Friday of that week, I spied on Naomi, watching from the window as she jumped on her horse and rode off after preparing our last meal of the day. I didn't have to ask where or what. The next day the pleasure of the previous evening was evident in her face. She had never been lovelier. With skin as smooth as the petals of magnolia blossoms, she had a rosy glow about her. Her dark eyes sparkled like gemstones. Naomi's long tresses, which she usually tied back from her face, fell freely about her shoulders. Clearly, the poor girl was in love.

Arabelle told me earlier that she'd visited with her, even pleaded, warning of the failings of all men. "Naomi appeared to be someplace else. I don't think she understand a word I say."

"We must not let this man ruin her," I said.

"I have no potion to combat such as this. It be as God intended, uncontrollable."

"Why?"

"To continue the species. That all it be. That what so much is about. Not good or evil, simply survival."

How I marveled at the wisdom of my friend. The brilliance of her mind far exceeded my own. Still, the problem with Naomi unsettled me. I couldn't idly stand by, so finally one early morning, I confronted her again with nothing new, just the same rhetoric I'd offered before. "Naomi, if you continue on this path, you'll end up with another child. I'm not sure Garland will allow that."

"What would that have to do with him? Such a situation would only concern me and my own future husband."

How could she possibly be so naïve? If she'd been still a child, I would have taken her by the shoulders and shaken her.

Since that wasn't possible, cruel words were the only weapon available to me. "No matter what Jonathan says, he won't marry you. He'll have you, and then leave you behind."

She answered my advice with a cold stare that chilled my bones. "It was you who taught me to believe in some possibility for myself. You praised my beauty, my intelligence, my ability to work and create. If I'm making a mistake about this, it will be your own fault, for if you had not told me first, I wouldn't have believed Jonathan when he told me how lovely and capable he found me to be. He says he'll never be satisfied with anyone else, no matter how handsome a dowry some other woman might possess."

My brain whirled. Somehow I had to make her face the truth. "All men lie, Naomi. They lie, perhaps, not so much out of evil, but instead to get what they feel they must have. Arabelle calls it survival."

Knowing I could do no more to convince her, I left her out by the chestnut tree, hoping my warning would save her. Saddened that I lacked ammunition strong enough to combat the force of her will, I went back inside to see to the children, those blessed little ones who belonged to both of us.

Lacking a way to save Naomi, I prayed for her daily, leaving her fate with God. My heart lifted briefly when two weeks later she showed up at the meeting house. I watched as she bowed her head, a pensive look on her face. One Quaker and then another rose speaking their hearts. Perhaps Naomi had something to say.

I prayed she would arise, breaking the silence by revealing what troubled her heart. Instead she spoke not a word and left quickly, as soon as the meeting ended.

The next meeting, when Jonathan showed up there with her, they were met by stares and whispers. Though such rude reactions were contrary to my liberal Quaker beliefs, I did believe that Jonathan had no business there among us. Garland, livid and beside himself, threatened to speak with Naomi again.

Twenty-Eight

Though I swore after Nellie died that I'd never go looking for anyone who lived across the river where I had no business, I could think of nothing else as the days grew warmer. I felt as desperate to save Naomi as I had seven years before when I'd gone searching for her, wanting to make sure she was properly cared for by her uncle.

My determination was fueled by the words of Hilda Lamb, an honorable woman, only a few years older than me, who attended our church. When she stopped by our house one March morning to bring us sassafras, I knew she had more on her mind than tea when she asked, "Is Naomi here?"

"She's working in the field. Garland and Arabelle too. We've all been working from dawn until dusk."

"I hate to trouble you, particularly now, but I learned something yesterday that I think you should know."

My heart didn't even skip a beat. I'd been expecting bad news ever since Jonathan showed up at the Friends' meeting. To keep my hands occupied, I picked up a piece of needlework

I planned to complete.

Though out of politeness, I expected Hilda to comment on the pretty birds I'd embroidered, she apparently remained too focused on gossip to notice.

"You should warn Naomi about that horrible man from across the river."

"I have."

"He's got to be stopped. He and his family care for the feelings of no one. I think we should bar him from coming to meetings."

"I doubt he'll be back."

Over the cup of tea, her gray eyes looked at me, accusing. "He's to marry someone else. "I have proof of it."

At first, I welcomed those words. That would stop Naomi, wouldn't it? But then I realized that Naomi had no way of winning. If Jonathan married someone else, her heart would surely break.

"What I tell you is in confidence," Hilda continued. "A friend— I will not mention her name but she often takes her carriage to Asheboro— claims that Jonathan is practically betrothed to the sister of his employer. Jonathan's mother encourages the union. The shop owner has never married, so his sister will receive a handsome dowry."

I shook my head, angry that a woman's lot in life depended so much on the money and possessions she brought to a union. How could possessions determine what kind of wife she might be? Yet, even in my own situation, I realized that Garland would never have married me if my father had not financed his dream of traveling here to North Carolina to make our home.

I asked many questions, yet after Hilda left, I still felt dissatisfied.

When everyone came inside for the big meal of the day, I

examined Naomi's face and realized she didn't know. Though tempted to tell her right away, I decided she'd never believe me without proof, so despite vowing never going across the river again, I knew I must.

Resorting to deception once again, the next morning, I requested that Arabelle spend the day with me instead of working in the field. Though I had no difficulty convincing Garland, Arabelle sensed something was awry. When finally I confessed my plan to her, she begged me not to go, but though my hands shook and my chest ached, nothing could stop me. For Naomi's sake, I had to saddle our horse and cross the river.

Hilda told me exactly where the shop was located, so it took me less than an hour to find it. Bone weary and frightened, I leaned against Samson when I dismounted. I could smell the animal's fear as well as my own. Burrowing my head into its mane, I prayed for strength and wisdom.

When I walked inside the store, a short man with a ready grin stood behind the counter. H asked what I needed. When I replied, "Just a bit of yarn for my sewing," he frowned.

People don't usually have time to shop for a single item. Still he feigned interest, asking what I planned on doing. As we chatted, a male customer came through the door, so the shopkeeper excused himself, saying, "Let me find my sister. She's more qualified to help you."

The woman who came through the door appeared to be at least as old as me. Her hair was a pretty shade of blonde but so thin that her scalp was visible in a few spots. Thin and fragile, her wan appearance reminded of a woman I'd known in Pennsylvania. After the woman died, it was whispered that she'd been addicted to laudanum.

As she displayed for me blue, green, yellow and red threads in multiple hues, she answered all questions politely. How could it be? Why would anyone choose this frail woman over someone as lively and capable as Naomi?

"I've been married for ten years and my plan is to make a special covering for a table. I want to embroider the date of our marriage and the dates of each of our children's births on it," I lied. "I'm not quite sure what motif I should use."

"Why not roses?" she asked.

I smiled, "Why, yes, roses might do quite well. Everyone likes them. What color roses would you suggest?"

"Some might advise red which signifies love. Others might select white for purity. I plan to carry pink ones."

"So you're getting married."

She blushed. With her head down, she nodded shyly.

"And who might the lucky man be?"

"He's asked that we keep it a secret."

"Really? Well, I wish you much happiness, my Dear," I said before requesting a ball of yellow yarn.

"Did you decide against roses?" she asked.

"Simple daisies, I believe will be more to my liking."

My back hurt as I began my ride back home. Before I reached the rickety bridge that joined the two sides of the river, I came upon a group of men, gathered around a fire. When I viewed their red faces, I decided they were probably drunk. They made rude comments and chuckled. One yelled out at me, "Get over here, Sister, I've got something to show you." Another added, "Maybe you got something to show us as well."

I hit Samson hard, hurrying him along.

Once home, I sipped a bit of broth Arabelle brought to me but refused to answer any of her questions. After writing a note to Garland, letting him know I'd taken to my bed, I wearily climbed the stairs. Crawling under the covers, I prayed that all the messiness involving Naomi would soon disappear.

Twenty-Nine

I had no idea what to do to end the mess. Going to Naomi wouldn't help. Neither would telling Garland. The secret I'd learned of Jonathan's engagement sickened me. Worse, I had no actual proof, for I'd failed to get a confirmation from the woman that her betrothed was indeed Jonathan Lewis.

As anxious as I might be to protect Naomi, I realized I had an even bigger responsibility, looking after my own health for the sake of my unborn child.

Nevertheless Naomi's predicament continued to eat at me until the following Friday when I received an unexpected package. Opening it, I found the china that had once belonged to my mother. The dishes had been shipped six months before. I picked up each piece, studying the floral pattern of lilies hugging the rim of each cup and plate. As I took the china from the box, I recalled so much about my mother. In some ways, she reminded me of Naomi. Spontaneous, she always had several projects going at once: her needlework, cooking elaborate cakes, growing new flowers in her garden. Despite my father's distain, she opened the doors of her home frequently to friends and family, welcoming them warmly, a flush of excitement tinting her cheeks pink. She had no traces of my own starchiness. I'd inherited that trait from my father.

Should I store the new dishes, keeping them for special occasions? That certainly seemed a practical thing to do, but something in me so desperately longed for change. I was tired of the old me, unable to bear a child, unable to communicate freely with my husband, unable to touch Naomi's heart, breaking down the wall between us, getting to the core of her, the enchanting child-like person who had willingly shared her children with me.

Suddenly, I found myself taking the old tin plates, many of them dented; all dull from wear, from the shelves. Carefully, I replaced them with dishes which would be a reminder of my mother every time we ate from them. Somehow the very sight of those plates and cups stretched my mind and lifted my spirit. As a Quaker, I should shun possessions, but those dishes stirred up wonderful recollections of my mother. Briefly I was there in Pennsylvania again as I recalled only the best times.

When Arabelle entered the house, exhausted from the heat, she caught me singing a song, one I recalled from childhood. She lifted her head, her eyes bright. "Why, you be glowing," she said. "Today you be bright as them lightning bugs children catch."

When I showed Arabelle the dishes, she praised them highly.

"Would you like my old ones?" I asked.

Taken aback when she shook her head, muttering, "No, M'am." I couldn't fathom why my offer didn't please her.

Perhaps it had to do with her beliefs, which no matter how often she explained them to me, never became entirely clear to my mind. I recalled how long ago, while still in Pennsylvania, I'd read about Roman and Greek gods. There were so many of them, I could never keep them straight. Arabelle's beliefs were just as confounding.

When I walked to where she sat, offering her a gourd filled with cool water, the corners of her mouth turned up. "Naomi should have your old dishes," she said. "That child needs things of her own."

I frowned. "She no longer speaks to me."

"That don't mean she don't love you."

I turned away to pack up the tin plates and cups.

"Naomi be like all of us. She needs to have things that belong only to her."

The anger I'd been holding at bay spewed out. "The man Naomi wants will not marry her. His intentions are to marry another woman."

"Does Naomi know?"

"She never listens when I warn her. Wild and reckless, she's always been. Wild and reckless she'll always be."

"Why she be so wild and reckless? What be the reason?"

Arabelle's words caught me off guard. Too stunned to answer, I walked to the nearest chair and sat down.

"That child never had a single day of freedom." Arabelle shook her head when she said it. "I spect that be gnawing on her. Freedom be worth most anything. When I came seeking it, I knew I might die and my children might die, but I keep walking down the road anyway. Nothing, except being carried back, could have stopped me or my husband. Freedom. That be what he wanted too."

I studied Arabelle's face. "Your life here is so hard," I said.

"Often you work from sunup until sundown."

"Hard work can be endured, even be a good thing cause something be accomplished from it. But if there be no freedom, there be no chance to give yourself credit. Nasty worms might as well chew on your soul."

Arabelle made sense. I could not keep Naomi safe, for it wasn't my right. Though I thought of her hope chest as a "hopeless chest," to her it meant possibility.

In that moment, I recalled my own predicament. I'd wanted children more than anything, but each past pregnancy failed. Naomi allowed me to have her children, to love, to care for. She'd given me the greatest possible gift. Though it had originally been Arabelle's idea, not my own, I suddenly wanted nothing more than for Naomi to have my old tableware. Closing my eyes, I prayed, though I couldn't imagine how it could ever be, that the orphan would one day have her own house and husband.

I arranged with Garland to let Naomi and Arabelle stop working in the field early on Friday. Reluctantly, he agreed. Arabelle had gathered up and made a few items for Naomi and besides the old dishes, I found other articles around the house that we didn't need. I also took from my shelves a jar of blackberry jam. The stone of remorse that burdened my heart had finally desolved. I decided that I would also give the embroidery piece I'd been working on to her.

Though I had earlier invited Naomi to tea, she insisted on going to her place first to freshen up. After Arabelle and I waited nearly an hour for her, we became concerned. "I'll go check on Naomi while you brew our tea," I said to Arabelle."

I knocked on Naomi's door. No one answered, so I walked to the back of her place. Hearing whispers, I stood silent for a moment, then I heard Jonathan's voice. "A week from today," he said. "Meet me at the river."

Stooping behind a bush, hoping to remain hidden, I inhaled deeply to slow the rapid beating of my heart. It seemed an eternity, but must have been only a minute, before I heard the whinny of Jonathan's horse. As he galloped away, I crept back to the front of Naomi's house. When I heard her walk back inside, I waited a few more minutes before knocking again.

When she answered, a puzzled look distorted her pretty face. "Is something wrong?"

"Why, no," I answered. "Arabelle and I are just anxious for you to see the surprises we have for you."

"What surprises?"

"The two of us had a long discussion. We decided that since you said you were going to get married, we should accept it. I received the dishes that belonged to my mother. I've decided that you should have my old ones; that is, if you'd like them."

I was surprised at how quickly she let down her guard, smiling sweetly as a child who'd been handed a piece of candy. Arabelle found some things for you as well. Please come over before the tea cools.

As we walked together across the yard, I marveled at how a few kind words had apparently smoothed our festering relationship. After entering the house, the three of us, each so different, joined hands. A soothing scent of lavender softened the air. Naomi fawned over my the old tinware. She thanked me, too, for the silver thimble I gave her and the jar of blackberry jam. When I offered her the table cover I'd embroidered, she refused. "It's too much. More than I deserve."

"Take it, child," Arabelle advised. "Don't refuse anything

offered for your hope chest. Now when that wedding gonna be?"

She blushed. "I promised I wouldn't tell," she said. "Jonathan says we must keep it a secret, but soon."

As I served us tea in the beautiful cups decorated with lilies, I touched my stomach. Naomi glanced at me. When we sat down, she grinned. "I pray every evening that you and the child you now carry will have a safe journey over the next few months. You were meant to be a mother."

Grateful for her words, I bowed my head. When I glanced back up, I took a good look at Naomi. Her face seemed fuller, rounder. Could it be? Was she also with child?

When I glanced at Arabelle, I realized she already knew. Turning away, to avoid Naomi's eyes, I almost asked, but when she turned to the side, saying to Arabelle how much she enjoyed the tea, I understood. Naomi didn't wish me to know, and this time, no matter how tempting, I wouldn't barge ahead.

Arabelle gave Naomi a basket she'd made of reeds. In it, she'd placed herbs, potions and salves.

"How good it feels to be sitting here with the two of you again," Naomi said. "I never had a brother or sister and barely knew my mother. The two of you are the closest to family I've ever known."

A bit of light caught a tear glistening in the corner of her eye. The sight of it tugged at my heart. All that I'd held against her, and all that I'd held against my husband seemed to lift up, rising like smoke. I finally understood the inevitable: Other dark clouds would blow my way, but despite whatever misfortune would befall me or Arabelle or Naomi, we would always cherish this bright moment of sisterhood.

Thirty

During the next week, Naomi appeared happy and content. Garland commented on how hard she worked, and Arabelle praised me for reaching out to the orphan despite the awkwardness of our situation. Though she spent most of the day in the fields, Naomi now left a bit of time at dusk to be with the children. On pleasant afternoons, I'd sit outside watching Davey and Mary romp about playing games such as hiding from one another or seeing how far they could toss stones. Like their birth mother, they, too, took to collecting some of nature's treasures in a basket.

One afternoon, noticing that Naomi looked utterly exhausted, I insisted that she and the children pause for a story. As I read to them, she watched as I placed my finger beneath each word. How I wished I'd continued with her reading lessons. Though she learned quickly, remaining focused was always difficult for her. Still, when it came to speaking, she excelled. She spoke as well as Garland and me, no longer shortening or leaving out necessary words as was the habit of those on the other side of the river.

Naomi was not all I'd wished, but gradually I accepted what she'd become. That, I believe, was the greatest gift I ever gave her. Though curious about her planned marriage, I asked for no details. Still, in my heart, I never believed there would be an actual ceremony. Perhaps when Jonathan married the older woman, Naomi, finally free of him, would become one of us again.

The smooth course of the previous week ended on Monday. The clock hands were on eight; Naomi had not shown up. Agitated, Garland had left for the field an hour earlier with Arabelle following behind. Soon as she gets here, I'll send her out to see to the chickens, I promised.

Noon arrived and still no sign of Naomi. Deciding to check on her, I put the children down for their nap, and walked to her tiny one-room cabin. I knocked and called out. No one answered. Where might she be? The door had been left unlatched, so, after taking a deep breath to calm myself, I walked inside. When I spotted the old trunk containing her hope chest, I smiled. When I realized she'd probably left to be with Jonathan, my grin disappeared.

There was nothing else I could do. At least, that's what I believed then. But during every day that followed, I questioned the wisdom of my decision. Could I have done anything to prevent the horrible catastrophe that befell Naomi? I suppose my conscience will deal with that question for as long as I live.

Going back home, I prepared the big meal of the day, roasting potatoes in coals, slicing red luscious tomatoes to go with the beans which had been simmering all morning. When Garland came in, his face reddened by both the sun and anger, I attempted to calm him down. After eating quickly, he said he needed to return to the fields. Arabelle had already left for

Naomi Wise A Cautionary Tale

her shanty to eat with her children.

Later, less than an hour before dusk, I became so disturbed by Naomi's disappearance, I paced the floor, and then called to the children. "Let's go find, Naomi," I said, forcing cheerfulness into my voice.

To them, it was like a game. As we walked, April wind whipped through my hair. When we neared Arabelle's place, I spotted her outside, her arms raised above her head. With eyes closed, Arabelle chanted while turning slowly around and around. The children, unafraid, ran to the tall woman. Like her, they, too, lifted their arms and circled. Arabelle, obviously in a trance, behaved as if no one else was there.

When the sun disappeared behind a dark cloud, she finally opened her eyes. I expected her to ask, "Where's Naomi?" She didn't. Her magic, I suppose, had already revealed the answer. She lifted Little Mary in her arms. She took Davey's hand. "Some things can't be changed," she said.

"Arabelle, you'll frighten the children."

She stared at me without speaking for several seconds. Finally, she suggested I take Davey and Mary home.

"No," I said. "I intend to find Naomi."

"Take the children home," she repeated.

The children ran a few paces away but suddenly stopped. Mary sobbed as if her heart were broken. Davey ran back to me.

"What?" I asked.

"Mama, we heard an awful scream."

I looked at Arabelle. She shook her head. "Can't nothing be done now. Go get your husband."

But I didn't. Instead, I ordered Arabelle to keep the children, before I took off running toward the river.

"Don't go there," she yelled.

When I reached the river bank, I glanced upstream and

then downstream. Some distance away, I spotted someone riding a black horse. Jonathan, I thought. Before the figure disappeared, I called out, "Naomi, Naomi." Walking to the edge of the bank, I spotted a body submerged in shallow water where weeds grew.

I don't remember the rest, but later Arabelle told me that she left with the children for my house to find Garland. By that time, he had already headed out with two other men who'd heard Naomi's screams as well as my own. By the time they arrived, I was unconscious.

When my husband lifted me up, I opened my eyes. "Look after, Naomi," I said. "She's in the river."

He relayed the message to the two men and then carried me home. After removing my wet dress, he gently tucked me into bed.

Until the day I die, there will always be questions. Could I have prevented Naomi's death? Was she fated by birth or mindset for disaster?

Garland furnished details when he returned. When the two men pulled Naomi from the river, her pale blue dress covered her face. When they pulled the dress down, they noticed dark bruises on her throat.

I interrupted. "It had to be Jonathan. I saw his black horse in the distance. Why did he kill her, Garland?"

My husband's chin dropped so low it grazed his chest. "The men say that Naomi's stomach was extended. They believe she was with child."

Getting up out of the bed, I leaned against the wall until I reached the washbowl. Bending over it, I threw up until nothing was left but dry heaves. When I could speak again, I asked, "Where are the children? "Do they know?"

"Not yet. I took them to the Hilliards to stay the night.

We'll tell them in the morning.

"Where's Arabelle?"

He turned away from me. "She's with Naomi. People from far and near came to the river, many carrying candles. They're down there now, praying and singing."

"I must go. I must see if there's anything I can do." As I spoke I felt as if I had floated out of my own body. I remained too high above my physical self for sorrow to overtake me. Later Naomi's death would break my heart.

"Considering your condition, it would be best for you to stay here, Mary Ruth."

"I need to go so I can protect Naomi from the vicious tongues of other women. While she was alive and vital, they gossiped about her being an orphan, which was no fault of her own. Whatever mistakes she made were almost inevitable. How can you and I blame her for any wrong thing she did. She gave us her two blessed children. If she had not, they, too, would have been orphans, following the sad path of their mother. Because of her generosity, we have a family. We have the children that God failed to give us."

My husband left the room while I dressed. When he returned, he asked, "Are you sure you're well enough?"

My eyes implored him. Well or not, I intended to go. Some things must be done. This was one of them. I took my basket from the shelf, filling it with the some of the sweet smelling lavender I'd dried in the way Nellie taught me. By the time we reached the river's edge, candles had been stuck in the ground surrounding Naomi's body. Women, some white, some black, slowly circled around her, chanting Omi Wise, Omi Wise, Poor ole Omi Wise.

The sight touched my heart. Tears streaked down my face. Scattering dried lavender as I walked, I joined the circling women. What would happen to Naomi's body? How would

I tell her children? How could we make sure that Jonathan Lewis was punished for this crime? The answers to those questions remained as distant as the stars above our heads.

That night I chanted not only for Naomi, but for all women whose lives had been unduly destroyed. Finally, so exhausted I could no longer stand without assistance from Arabelle, I returned home with Garland.

How radically Naomi's public image changed after she died. Previously she'd been a young woman virtually ignored. Suddenly everyone claimed to know so much about her. Some painted pictures of her, portraits of how they remembered her or how they believed she looked. Others composed songs, which they sang in mournful voices. In North Carolina, her fate became known as far west as the mountain peaks and as far east as the ocean's shore. Mothers, in stern whispers, related the cautionary tale of Naomi to their daughters, in hopes of keeping them celibate.

Years later, even a road and a bridge in our community were named for the poor girl who had no prospects.

Yes, like a star on a dark night, the memory of Naomi rose, bright, shining. I was touched when I discovered how much she'd meant to Davey and Mary, neither of them suspecting she was their mother. They spoke of her often.

One breezy afternoon, when Mary caught a butterfly, she ran to show me. "It's Omi," she said smiling. "It's Omi come back to be with us." Many times I heard Davey talking when no one was there. Once he said, "I'm sorry I did that." Another time, "I'm being a good boy just for you." Sometimes, he included his mother's name in these conversations. Once I heard him plead, "Where are you, Omi?"

Putting my arms around both children, I assured them. "Naomi's in a good place, a beautiful place filled with trees and flowers and butterflies. She's happy there."

"Can we go too, Mama?" Davey asked.

I bit my lip to stall tears. "Surely, Davey. We'll all go there some day, but, for now, your Papa and I need you here with us."

Though Garland and I never fully comprehended Arabelle's belief system, we knew it brought her peace. Perhaps because she'd experienced so much grief in her own life, she accepted Naomi's death philosophically. Sometimes she compared the orphan to passion flowers which bloomed rarely but spectacularly in the woods, then died by nightfall. Other times, I noticed her crossing herself as she prayed to Naomi.

After Naomi's demise, Garland aged. Within a month after her passing, his hair turned entirely gray and the sharp blue of his eyes faded. Always a quiet man, he rarely spoke any more. I feared his spirit would never lift again, but finally, in my eighth month of pregnancy, when I gave birth to a small hearty boy, who bellowed whenever he didn't immediately receive whatever he wanted, the miracle of birth rekindled the light within Garland's breast, as well as my own.

Our miracle baby, weighting no more than three Irish potatoes, became our new beginning. We named him Adam.

Thirty-One

On April 18, 1809 the Randolph County Superior Court returned a bill for murder against Jonathan Lewis, and set the trial for October 27. The county coroner determined that Naomi was indeed pregnant. Because of the bruises, he surmised she had been violently pushed in the river where she drowned. Though Jonathan claimed to be innocent, the sheriff took him to jail.

His own people, those living on the other side of the river, protested his guilt. None of us believed a word of it. I, myself, had witnessed a person on a black horse, leaving the scene. In my very soul, I knew it could have been no one else, no one except Jonathan. His motive I believed was that he had promised to wed Naomi but had also promised to wed another. Spirited Naomi, I felt sure, would never let him get away with deserting her.

They held him in jail for six months, when with the help of the Sheriff and three other men, he escaped. The elusiveness of judgment during those times always astounded me. Though my thoughts were consumed with his being out there, perhaps even plotting to do harm to me and my family, there was little I could do. Taking care of the new infant took most of my time. Like a hawk, I hovered constantly over Adam, as if by sheer will I could shoo away the dark force that stole my other wee ones.

Now, looking back, I consider my situation at the time to be fortunate. If I had not remained so busy caring for my family, thoughts of the harm Jonathan had already caused combined with the possibility of even more destruction would have surely driven me mad. Arabelle fussed at me for refusing to let go of my hatred for Jonathan. When she said, "Evil is mighty; its strength grows when dwelled upon," I accepted the wisdom of her words, but the vision of Naomi's lifeless body, still clinging to my memory, made forgiveness impossible.

The day of Adam's first birthday, Arabelle reached for my hand and turned it over. Her index finger traced a line in my palm. "You'll live long and well," she said. Then she turned her attention to the area around my thumb. "Take care of yourself, Mary Ruth, for you will mother at least two more."

Soon as she made the prediction, I realized I had missed my monthly bleed at least twice. I tried to suppress the joy rising up within me. God willing, my next child would be healthy as Adam.

Indeed, I did give birth to two more babes, both boys as sturdy as Adam. Our second son Aaron had brown eyes like my own and sandy hair. The third, Daniel, who was two years younger, resembled Garland. Our house became a joyful place, filled with the laughter of children.

Arabelle, though crippled by arthritis, still helped on the farm. Her children worked in the field as well, until grown, then they escaped with the Underground Railroad, heading out to Canada where they would not be persecuted for the color of their skins.

My heart ached for her. The loss of one's children, no matter how young or old they might be, devastates the spirit. Their absence became a deep wound to her, one that could not be healed by her own magic. We both spoke and prayed for them daily. We took comfort in knowing that across the border, her children would be afforded opportunities unavailable to them in America.

How surprised I was when one afternoon in the fall of 1811, my kind-hearted neighbor Edith Hilliard came bearing news. As she sipped the mint tea I poured, she reported what she had learned earlier in the day. When her husband Thomas took corn to be ground at the grist mill, the owner told him that Jonathan Lewis had finally been captured in another state, where he had married and fathered a child. "I understand they plan to bring him back here for trial," she said. After placing her tea cup back on the table, she dabbed the corners of her mouth with a napkin.

I wasn't quite certain if the rivulet of tears flowing from my eyes was for joy or sorrow. Even hearing the scoundrel's name caused a pain in my chest, making it difficult to breathe.

Eventually, Jonathan was brought back to the Randolph County jail. Over a year later, he finally went on trial at the courthouse in Greensboro. The judge there charged him with escaping jail, but not killing Naomi Wise.

The corruptness of our justice system mystified me. How could they simply disregard the murder charge that had previously been made? All the dark thoughts I'd previously harbored about the man who callously destroyed Naomi, returned. Despite being a good Quaker woman who valued the life of every human being, I did not view Jonathan human.

If a poisonous snake coiled ready to strike me or someone I loved, I would not have hesitated to chop its head off with a hoe. Jonathan, I believed, deserved no better.

After I pleaded with him for several days, Garland finally relented, taking me to Greensboro, so that I could plead for Jonathan Lewis to be tried for murder. As we neared Greensboro in our buggy, I was surprised at how much the terrain had changed since those many years ago, when Garland and I first came to North Carolina. Civilization had supplanted too much of nature's beauty. Groves of trees had been cut down to make room for buildings and houses. We even viewed a few people out and about. As we passed by, they waved and smiled. Were they aware of the sad fate of Naomi Wise? Did they know that the man who killed her was in their jail?

I planned what I would say to the judge, but once we gained admittance to his office, he cautioned me. "Mrs. Eversole, your belief that Mr. Lewis committed murder is irrelevant."

"So," I said, a hot blush of anger warming my face, "killing a young woman is irrelevant. What if Naomi had been your wife or daughter, Your Honor?"

He bowed his head, covering his eyes with his hand, and for no good reason banged his gavel on the table in front of him.

Swiftly, so he would not see my tears, I turned, leaving.

Though the judge could keep me from testifying, he could not bar me from attending the trial, so two days later, I sat in the courtroom beside Garland and our sympathetic neighbors, Edith and Thomas Hilliard. Fearful of what the judge might do if I showed the least bit of emotion, I managed to bear up for most of the proceedings. Garland held my hand, squeezing it hard as the Judge declared, "Mr. Lewis, for escaping from jail, you will be incarcerated. No other charges will be brought against you."

Though Garland grabbed my arm, I managed to shake free of him and rise up. My knees shook as I shouted out so everyone in the courtroom would hear, "Jonathan Lewis, you killed Naomi Wise. Until my dying days, I'll know and you'll know it."

There were gasps. The judge banged his gavel. "Mr. Eversole, please escort your wife from the courtroom." I hid my face when Jonathan, his lips drawn up in a salacious grin, turned to look at me.

The murderer left North Carolina for Indiana soon after his release from jail. I heard a rumor that his own people quickly grew tired of his thieving and whoring, so ran him off. At least there was the comfort that he would be living far away. Though I could never open my heart enough to pray for his redemption, almost daily I offered up requests for the protection of his poor wife.

Eventually thoughts of Jonathan faded here in our community, but Naomi would never be forgotten. Children, even as young as six, knew the sad story of the orphan's death.

For several years, the two children birthed by the orphan remained with us, as close to us as our own. At age sixteen, Mary married Dale Hilliard, our neighbors' oldest son and moved less than three miles away.

Arabelle and I remained close as sisters. As long as she was able, she helped me in the house. Davey and later Adam worked alongside the two strong black men, Jessup and Abram, whom Garland hired to help with the crops and animals.

Eventually, I wholeheartedly accepted Arabelle's gift for healing. I'd witnessed with doubt as she talked warts off my children's hands. Perhaps they would have disappeared anyway, I thought. But one cold winter afternoon, as I placed more wood on the fire, my dress caught fire. After putting the fire out with her hands, Arabelle did her best to calm me. As she removed my clothing, I watched as blackened areas of the skin on my legs fell away. When she touched my wounds, speaking softly, asking that the fire be taken out of me and given to her, I winced with pain. Miraculously, by the next day, the burns began to heal.

Thirty-Two

I have heard it said of older couples that they grow to know one another so well they can eventually read one another's minds. Such never happened with Garland and me. He harbored many secrets and I accepted such, for I fought for the freedom of my own thoughts as well. Still we lived together and prospered. Though not the type of romantic relationship one reads of in books, we respected and helped one another.

   At age forty-three, while returning from the field one sunny afternoon, Garland collapsed, his body falling to the ground. Davey rode off for the doctor, who arrived at our house by nightfall. By midnight, Garland was more comfortable. According to Doctor Odom, the problem was my husband's heart. After bleeding him, taking at least a pint of blood from his body, the young physician spoke to me softly, warning that Garland might never be able to go to the field and work again. Remembering how I'd been told by a doctor that I'd never birth a healthy child, I took those words with a grain of salt.

Arabelle sniffed as if she smelled something putrid when I explained the treatment Garland received. "Bleeding, now how that be helping? Mr. Eversole need to eat collard greens and yams instead of hog meat. He need to calm his soul, too. A heart be weakened by what a man do. Also by what he thinks."

I never mentioned Arabelle's advice for my husband appeared to grow stronger day by day. Finally, one morning, less than a month later, during our first meal of the day, he announced, "I'll be getting back to the garden today."

"Why not leave the heavy work to the children," I suggested.

"I want to be there," he said. "A farmer. That's what I am. If I can't farm, what use am I?"

I argued with him. Still, he appeared well again. The paleness of his face had been replaced with a ruddy glow. He walked again in long easy strides, no longer depending on a cane.

Before noon, Davey ran back to the house, tears streaming down his face.

I knew even before he said, "It's Papa."

We buried Garland near the edge of the field beneath one of our chestnut trees. I still visit him there every day. Sometimes, I speak to him about the sealed note he left for me, the one Mary held onto for a month after he died.

When finally, Mary reluctantly gave the note to me, I read it again and again, letting the words seep into my brain until I memorized every word.

Dearest Mary Ruth,

   I have wanted to be a good husband to you and a good Quaker here in this community, but I failed. As you already know, I fathered Mary. I shared this fact with her before entrusting her with this message for you.

I apologize here, once again, for hurting you, but as for the actual betrayal, I've never been able to imagine avoiding it. I lost all reason, perhaps my faith as well, the day I took Naomi in my arms.

And there is another secret, one far more shameful. I killed Naomi's uncle. I killed him because I feared what he might do to her and our family. Arrogance never allowed me to confess it while alive. How I wish I had been brave enough to do so, for the burden of my sin eats always at my soul.

I worry that you might somehow find yourself accountable for my dastardly actions. Please do not. Though I always prided myself on being a good man, a man in control, the qualities I deemed as assets ended up being my Achilles heel. Pray for me. Take care of our children. They, along with you, have been the bright lights of my life.

Love, Garland

After ripping the note into tiny pieces and tossing them into the fireplace, a cloud of sadness hovered over my spirit. Why hadn't I recognized the darkness that overtook my husband? If I'd known, perhaps I could have helped. Knowing another's heart, I have concluded, is the most perplexing problem we face while living on this earth. Knowing our own heart is difficult enough.

Garland's wise words, "Take care of our children," have guided my steps since his death. By doing so, I've been amply rewarded. Each of them is different, with individual talents and flaws, but they love one another, and me as well, I believe. Not a one of them has proved a disappointment.

My youngest son Daniel died of pox before he reached his fifteenth birthday. The others, Davey, Mary, Adam, and

Aaron still embrace Garland's dream of living off the land and seeking peace and tranquility here among Friends who share our beliefs.

Thirty-Three

We'd all worked especially hard during 1816, so we looked forward to celebrating the spring of 1817. The trees on our property were bounteous and green again. Wild flowers splashed the meadow with color when our family gathered for Easter on April 6.

Aaron captured the turkey we ate that year. Mary asked the blessing. Since Garland's death, Davey, who had become the patriarch of our family, making all the major decisions concerning the farm, carved the turkey and led us in singing.

A perfect day I believed, but as time has taught me, perfect rarely exists.

That evening Davey came to me. The serious expression on his face warned me that all was not well. "Mother, would you consider sparing me from the farm for a few weeks?"

Deeply disturbed by his question, I feared, at first, he might be ill. "The farm belongs to you and your siblings. You need not ask me."

Davey kissed me on the cheek. "I'll stay if my going troubles you, but the light within me, which you speak of so eloquently, urges me to do its bidding."

"Just what might your mission be?"

When he explained that he wished to visit Jonathan Lewis, now living off in Indiana, my blood ran cold. I turned from him, wishing to hear no more.

"I need to do this for Naomi," he said. I've heard reports that Jonathan is near death. Perhaps he will confess."

"I fear for you," I said. "What do you plan to say to that dreadful man?"

"I will tell him that whether he admits it or not, our family knows he killed my blood mother."

Despite my apprehensions, I greatly admired Davey's intention to speak out on behalf of Naomi.

I prayed for my son every day until he returned to us from his visit to Jonathan Lewis' home in Clark County, Indiana. I still remain grateful for having my prayer answered. When he arrived on the fifth day of May, all of us stopped work long enough to welcome him. Even Arabelle joined us for a spring meal on the lawn.

After feasting on pork and yams, we gathered outside for tea and the thin butter cookies Davey brought back from Indiana.

I sensed a new lightness in my son—the effortless way he walked about, the big hugs he bestowed on each of us. He even whistled a tune as he waited for each of us to settle down.

"I've waited long enough for what you have to tell us," I declared. "My heart will stop beating if I have to wait a second longer."

The younger children, well acquainted with my keyed-up emotions, giggled.

He winked. "I'll not tell a word of it, not until I finish Arabelle's wonderful tea."

Standing, I refilled his cup. By then all of us were anxiously anticipating the news.

"When I arrived at Jonathan's modest house," he finally said, "a woman answered the door." Davey described how she appeared ill-used, her clothes in tatters. "When I requested to see Mr. Lewis, she revealed he was her husband. Then, shaking her head, she said, 'He'll deny your entrance through our door. His younger brother is with him and a cousin. He wishes no other company.'"

"I whispered to her, wishing no one else to hear. 'Wouldn't you like to know the truth?'"

"She bit her lower lip, saying not a word for a moment or two. Then she looked me in the eye. 'What I would like,' she said, 'is to see my husband die in peace.'"

"You turned the charm on her, didn't ya, Davey?" Mary asked.

He blushed.

Impatient to hear all that transpired, I suggested we should let Davey get on with it.

"Though I've seen others on their deathbed, I've never seen anyone look quite as miserable as Jonathan. His face, red as a ripe plum, made him appear as if he the fires of hell had already settled in his body. His breathing remained shallow, and most curious of all, his eyes bulged out, making me think they might pop right out of his head. Though I came there, not expecting to feel one dram of sympathy for his cursed soul, I walked over, touching his hand, and asked,

'How you feeling, Jonathan?'"

"He raised his head from the pillow and asked, 'Who in blazes might you be?'"

"When I told him I was Naomi's son, he rubbed his eyes and stared again."

"Do you think he believed you?" I interrupted.

"I'll never know," Davey said, before continuing his tale.

"Bending over the bed, unable to escape the rotten stink of him, I asked the cruel question that had hung over our house for much of my life. 'Did you kill my mother? Did you kill Naomi Wise?'"

"He threw his head back, gazing at the ceiling. 'Oh, God, let me die,' he pleaded."

"Perhaps God will allow you to die in peace if you answer my question."

"One of the men threatened to throw me from the room, but then, Jonathan's wife went to to the dying man's side. Her words surprised me, for touching his swollen hand, she said, 'Jonathan, perhaps it's time to confess whatever's on your heart. You ain't got long.'"

"The words finally worked free of him. 'Yes, God forgive me, I killed Naomi Wise.'" That's exactly what he said. "Soon as he confessed, he relaxed, sinking back into the pillow. Before I had time to put my hat back on and leave, the death rattle began."

Bowing my head, I closed my eyes. "It's over," I said. The grams of bitterness within my own heart were finally melting.

Thirty-Four

On this day, here beneath the shady branches of the chestnut tree, I will complete my reminiscence of Naomi. Writing it has brought peace to my own soul these past few months and hopefully to the orphan's spirit as well.

Despite being a wild child, too often led by passion, I consider Naomi a champion among women. She refused to bow down to society's demands. Despite cruelty and heartbreak, she continued to laugh, sing, love, and cling to the belief that achievement was possible, even for a poor orphan deemed to have no prospects.

How I admire her and Arabelle, both capable and loving; both strong-willed and outspoken. These two women lifted me up, helping me find my own possibility. Without their encouragement, I would never have birthed children who lived. Without their inspiration, I would never have written these words.

I hope my true story of Naomi Wise will be a cautionary

tale, warning young women to be circumspect, careful of what they say and do. The consequences of our smallest indiscretions often remain with us until the day we die. Though Naomi wished harm to no one, her actions hurt others and regrettably resulted in her own death. She lived in an age when what might have been considered charming by some was viewed by others as vulgar, unacceptable.

Oh, yes, she should have behaved better, but in her defense, the poor child had no mother to guide her. Worse still, society found her wanting.

I hope my words will be a cautionary tale not only for impatient young women like Naomi, but also for those of us who have been around long enough to practice good manners and understand the conventions of society. We, too, often fail. Rather than listening and advising, we criticize. How easy to find fault with someone else. When our idle minds should be attempting to understand and help those unlike ourselves, too often we attempt to elevate ourselves by putting them down.

Naomi could not help she was an orphan, yet we shamed her for it. She was forced to beg for food and attempt to find a husband without benefit of a dowry. For a place to sleep and food to eat, she worked long hours without the slightest prospect of anything else. And what did we do? We watched, criticizing her, waiting for her to fail.

Anabelle was treated no better. Even when she escaped the tyranny of her slave owner, she gained only scant freedom. Still she cared for my family as if we were her own. Foolish doctors, with their antique notions failed me and the first three children I birthed. They failed Garland as well. Anabelle saved us and saves us still with the magic of her medicine. Society criticizes her for what they don't understand.

My dream if for a future time—a time I hope my children will live to see—when society uplifts the downtrodden, seeing

Sandra Redding

beneath the different skin colors and beyond the varying personalities, realizing they we are all more alike than we are different. We all have hearts that beat rapidly when excited and arms capable of reaching out, comforting one another. We have ears to listen and voices to say, "I understand." We also have the will to protest when we see injustice, and a bright light inside—a light to guide us, a light connecting us to God.